HARRIS COUNTY PUBLIC LIBRARY

Ward
Ward, H. M.
Second chances

$18.99
ocn890195349
First edition   09/09/2014

DISCARD

SECOND CHANCES

By

H.M. WARD
& STACEY MOSTELLER

H.M. WARD PRESS
www.SexyAwesomeBooks.com

COPYRIGHT

This book is a work of fiction. Names, characters, places, and incidents are either the product of the author's imagination or are used fictitiously, and any resemblance to actual persons, living or dead, events, or locales is entirely coincidental.

Copyright © 2014 by H.M. Ward
All rights reserved.

No part of this book may be reproduced, scanned, or distributed in any printed or electronic form.

H.M. WARD PRESS
First Edition: July 2014
ISBN: 9781630350314

Second
Chances

Dear Reader,

This is a story that I dreamed up a long time ago, and without the assistance of a coauthor it would have taken another year, or more, before it came to life. SECOND CHANCES was imagined by H.M. Ward (me) and then I handpicked Stacey Mosteller to help bring these characters to life. We've written this book together, and had a lot of fun doing so!

I have to admit that I'm a little nervous. This isn't like the other HM Ward books you've read. This is a tearjerker romance, as you noticed if you saw the video teaser. Grab your tissues and get ready.

I can't wait to hear what you think!

-HM Ward

Chapter 1

"Ma'am?" The officer is sitting beside me on my little couch, his eyes full of sympathy that I don't want to see. As soon as I opened the door, the pit of my stomach dropped and a chill raced up my spine, strangling me into silence. I know why he's here, standing tall with a second officer, both in dress blues. They are here to say the words no wife wants to hear, but he's yet to say them. First they introduced themselves, mild smiles on their faces, and asked to come in. Then they start down the slow path to reality, one that ends with a coffin. I know how this works. I know because it's something I've feared every time Cade deployed.

Just breathe. Staring blankly at Cade's huge television hanging across the room, I continue to hold the serene smile on my face, as if they are here for tea. The surreal nature of the moment needs to be shattered, but I can't do it.

"Ma'am, I'm afraid we're here with bad news," the chaplain starts again, putting a hand on my shoulder and startling me back to the present. "Is there someone we can contact for you so you won't be alone?"

I shake my head and keep my eyes fixated on the TV—the TV Cade wanted so badly, with the super huge screen and the super expensive HD whosie-whatsit that he thought was so cool. I never could see a difference. Cade stood in the store gaping and excitedly pointing, explaining why this one was better, how the screen was so much sharper even though they all looked the same to me. We had gone into the mall for a blender, and came out with this. Cade was beaming, practically bouncing up and down. It seemed like a better purchase, because no kitchen appliance in the world

SECOND CHANCES

would ever put that kind of smile on my face. Now the television sits there silently, its black screen mocking me.

I find my voice. "Just say it. I can't bear it any longer. I know why you're here. Just say it." My throat is so tight that the words sound strangled. I blink once, but I don't dare look at him.

His head lowers and he says the words I knew were coming. They float through the air and for a moment this seems like someone else's life, not mine. But his firm hand on my shoulder, the way he grips my arm and tips his head to the side to catch my eye makes me look at him. He says, "I'm sorry for your loss. Can I call someone?"

I shake my head. The one person I want is gone.

"Ma'am, if there's anything I can do—anything at all—please call." He hands me a card. I take it between my fingers, noticing the smoothness of the paper on my skin. Minutia rules in moments like these. The clock ticks louder, my breathing is labored and sounds like screams in my ears. A car rolls down the street roaring like a jet engine rather than an automobile. Another tick. Another tock. A drop of water from the faucet splashes in the sink deafeningly loud.

In a zombie-like state, I walk the men to the door and thank them. I smile and go through the motions like a robot. *Thank you for coming. Thank you for telling me. Thank you. Thank you. Thank you.*

Closing the door behind them, I lean back against it, my knees going weak as I remember how happy I was just a few hours ago. Today should be one of the most joyful days of my life, and instead, I'm preparing to tell everyone I know that Cade will never come home.

I knew something was wrong, but I wouldn't let myself worry. Things happen sometimes preventing his call. I kept telling myself it was nothing, but my stomach's been so queasy. Cade promised he would call me on Tuesday. I was grinning ear to ear since Monday night, practically bouncing up and down with news, but his call never came. Then, Wednesday and Thursday both passed without a call or even an email, but I still told myself that it was nothing. Plus my secret was burning a hole in my mouth. I had to tell him and I wanted to tell him first, so I waited—excited beyond measure—dreaming of a future that can never exist.

Pushing off the door, I walk over to the hallway table that sits by the phone. I look down at the tiny white stick that changes everything. One little word that would have made him so happy, and now he'll never know.

Suddenly, tears begin to roll down my cheeks in great globs. They fall so fast and furious, I can barely see. Picking up the pregnancy test, I clutch it to my chest as my legs give out and I sink to the floor. I pull my knees tightly into my chest and my head tips forward to rest on top of them. Bone crushing anguish races through my body as I hold fervently to that piece of plastic.

"I never got to tell him," I say to no one.

I glance at the stick again, staring at the one word that seemed like magic a few days ago.

PREGNANT.

H.M.WARD

Now this baby is all I have left of Cade, and our child will grow up never knowing his father.

Chapter 2

I don't know how long I sit on the floor in front of the phone, staring at the word *pregnant* glaring up at me. I barely move when my mother kneels down beside me, wrapping her arms around me and holding me tight. She murmurs nonsense into my hair as she rocks us back and forth, before noticing what I'm clutching in my hands.

"Oh honey!" she exclaims. "When did you find out?" Her excitement is palpable, even through both of our tears.

I don't understand how she can be happy right now, about anything. I was overjoyed about the baby when I first found out, but that happiness has been eclipsed by gut-wrenching grief. Instead of spending the next eight months sharing sonogram pictures, picking out baby names, and decorating a nursery with my husband, I will instead spend the next eight months knowing he won't ever see our baby.

He'll never hold him.

He'll never get to love him.

The only way my baby will know his daddy is from me telling him about him. That pains me so much that I can't think about it. We'd tried so hard for so long, that we thought a baby wasn't in the cards for us. Other couples pop out kids like Pop Tarts. Ding! Here's another! That wasn't the way it went for us. Years passed with no luck.

I slam my head back into the wall and let the tears streak down my face, not bothering to wipe them away. "Monday night. I never got to tell him, Mom. Now, he'll never know." Dissolving into sobs once more, whatever she says doesn't register. I melt into a puddle on the floor and curl into a ball. I can't stop crying. I want to stop, but the sobs won't let up. The next thing I know my dad's by my side, helping me stand, before they both walk me into the bedroom.

My mom pulls back the comforter and guides me onto the mattress. Kissing my forehead, she says, "Why don't you rest for a while. We'll start making phone calls and letting everyone know, okay?" Her voice breaks, and I can see Daddy wrapping his arms around her, much like she did for me earlier, and pain rips my chest in two.

Cade should be here. He should be hugging me while we whisper in bed, dreaming about things to come, our little family, and losing each other in kisses and hugs. Instead of preparing for that future, I will be planning his funeral. Instead of embracing this new life, I'm saying goodbye to his. Sorrow chokes me and I scream at the top of my lungs, "It's not true! He can't be gone! He promised me! Mom, he promised me!"

Her hand rests gently on my forehead as she strokes my hair away from my face. My body heaves as I sob into my pillows, screaming that this isn't fair, that it can't be true. This isn't my life. "They made a mistake. They must have. He was going to call, he was. He was…"

Mom sits there until I still and the tears slow. She says nothing. Sometimes there is nothing to say. Her aged hand strokes my brow over and over again, using the soothing touch that I remember so well from when I was a little girl. She stays until I'm finally calm, then kisses my cheek and slips out the door.

I've known Cade my entire life. We grew up next door to each other and were in the same classes all the way through elementary school. When I first started crushing on boys, he was the only one I noticed. Cade was my first kiss, my first and only love, my *everything*. I don't know how to live without him; he's been with me through everything, everyday, for years.

Turning over, I face the wall and shut my eyes, letting the tears continue to fall as I clutch his pillow to me, holding it the way I wish I were holding him. I keep one hand on my stomach, cradling the only part of him I have left. All I can think about is the fact that he's gone. I'll never see his smile or hear his voice, never feel the touch of his hand. Cade will never get to put his hand on my belly to feel the baby kick, he won't be here when this child is born, and we won't take our baby home together. I worry that my grief will hurt the baby, so I try to hold it together. I can't fall apart no matter how much I want to lay down and never get up again. This child needs me to be strong, and I wish I was.

As I lay on the bed we shared, I barely register the low tones of people talking on and off throughout the afternoon. Their voices carry in to the bedroom through the cracked door. Periodically, Daddy walks by and glances into the room, but he keeps his distance. The only way he knows to cure tears is with chocolate or dollies. The broken woman on the bed isn't a little girl anymore and no amount of toys will fix this. He paces away, back to the living room. They stay here in our little old house, making calls and preparing everything that needs to be done.

My tears fall freely, mourning the loss of my best friend, my husband, my *soul mate*. Finally, all the crying takes it's toll and I fall into a fitful sleep where I dream of the way things should have been.

Chapter 3

~TWO MONTHS PRIOR~

The sound of the bus that will take Cade's unit to the plane is drowned out by the sobs that are wracking my body. I promised myself that I wouldn't do this. I wouldn't send him off to war with the memory of me with a tear-stained face. We've been here before, this isn't his first deployment. But, I *don't* want to be here again. I don't know what I would do if I lost Cade, and that's all I've been able to think about for days.

My husband just finished training for his latest promotion at Lackland Air Force Base and now he's being sent back to Iraq. Because this base is close to both of our parents, when we decided to start our family, Cade wanted me to be closer to them—especially knowing accepting his most recent promotion meant he would be deployed soon. He wants our child to be closer to its grandparents than he was to his own growing up. We never considered the possibility that I wouldn't get pregnant right away, or that we'd still be trying years later.

Getting pregnant has been so much harder than we thought it would be. It's simple, right? Decide to have a baby, go off birth control, and boom—you're pregnant. Yeah, not so much. It's been a never-ending cycle over the past year of both hope and disappointment. I'm almost thirty-one years old and I'm afraid I'm never going to be a mom. Each time I've had to say goodbye to my husband, I panic thinking of stories I see all the time about other soldiers who've been killed in the line of duty. Losing Cade isn't the only thing that terrifies me. The idea of losing him and having nothing left of him? That's enough to break me for good.

Tears run unchecked down my cheeks as we prepare to say goodbye. A military goodbye is *nothing* like a normal trip goodbye. Each time he's deployed, we've said goodbye as though we'll never see each other again and it's so damn *hard*. Nothing is going the way it should lately, and him leaving so soon after finding out once again that I'm not having his baby makes it ten times more difficult.

"Oh, sweetheart, come here." Cade pulls me into his arms and hugs me tight. I wrap my arms around his neck as though I could keep him here with me by never letting him go. Inhaling deeply, I try to commit his scent to memory; it's a cross between his favorite cologne and the body wash he's been using since high school. It's my favorite smell in the world, and one I never want to forget.

Cade rubs my back soothingly as he murmurs, "It's okay, Genevieve. The next six months are going to fly by, and before you know it, you'll be back here picking me up so we can go home. This is nothing. Now, no more tears."

Reaching up, Cade pulls my arms away from the death grip they have on his neck and backs away from me slightly. Shaking his head, he smiles softly at me as he frames my face in his hands, using his thumbs to wipe the tears from my cheeks. Leaning forward he presses his mouth to mine. His tongue traces my lips and I open them in response, tangling my tongue with his, savoring our last kiss for the next few months.

Cade releases me and steps away. One corner of his mouth creeps up as he adjusts the sand colored bag on his shoulder. Looking at my husband standing in front of me, wearing his flight suit, a bag on his shoulder and another, bigger bag at his feet, I'm struck by just how handsome he is. He's tall, taller than me by about four inches, with blonde hair and eyes the color of melted chocolate. He's thin, just muscular enough to be hot but not *too* muscular, and his look hasn't changed much since we got married. He's filled out in some places, thinned down in others. He's definitely not that eighteen-year-old boy, but you'd never guess he was over thirty either.

Taking my hand, Cade pulls it up to his mouth and places a gentle kiss on my wedding rings. He bought them for me just after basic training and he was so nervous to propose. The engagement ring is white gold with one large stone in the middle, a smaller stone on either side and then tiny stones around the band. The wedding band matches, part of a set, and is covered in the same tiny stones. The kiss he places on my rings is our good luck charm. He's given me the same kiss on each deployment and he's come home every time.

Leaning in one final time, Cade wraps his arms around my middle, kissing my neck softly. Turning, I place my lips against his ear and whisper, "Maybe next time." It's been just over two weeks since the last negative test, and knowing he was going to be gone soon, we didn't try again.

Pulling away, he smirks at me, "Next time. And, even if it's not, we'll still have fun trying, babe." He runs the backs of his fingers down my cheek, his smile faltering just a little. "I love you, Genny. Don't ever forget that."

"I love you too, Cade." Then, together, we say the same thing we've said every deployment for luck. We have so many rituals for these goodbyes. "Twice as much as yesterday, but not half as much as tomorrow."

As he turns to grab his other bag so he can board the bus, my mom's arm wraps around me and hugs me close. Sighing, I lay my head on her shoulder, trying to smile for my husband. I don't want his last memory of me for the next few months to be tears running down my cheeks. I force the corners of my mouth up, though it probably looks more like I have gas than anything else.

Mom elbows me in the side and mumbles, "Smile, Genny."

I elbow her back, gently. "I am."

"You look constipated."

"So do you."

My mom's jaw drops mid-wave as she stares at me, which makes me smile.

Cade laughs. "Take care of her for me, okay?" He asks my mom. "Don't let her

SECOND CHANCES

worry, and make sure she stays busy. The next few months will fly by." She agrees, and before he walks away, he leans in for one last kiss. Mom blushes as she looks over her shoulder at us, like we shouldn't be so intimate in public.

Cade turns to me, kissing away one of the tears rolling down my cheek, "See you soon, baby."

Chapter 4

~TWO YEARS LATER~

I grab my cell as I leave the playground, my sweet baby asleep on my shoulder. He wore himself out.

"Hey, Lanie. What's up?"

Her voice is careful, with a forced carefree, I'm-not-checking-up-on-you tone. "Hey Gen! I'm just calling to see if we're still on for a little Genny/Lanie time." She blurts out a curse and I hear a horn blare.

"Yep and you shouldn't be talking while you're driving. You're going to get another ticket." I chide her a little as I get

SECOND CHANCES

to my car and open the door, carefully placing the baby into his seat. He stirs a little bit but doesn't wake. After I strap him in, I kiss his forehead lightly and shut the door.

"Okay, but in my defense, I was parked when the call started." Lanie sounds hesitant, which is strange for her. She's one of my best friends.

"That won't save you from a ticket. And, I know why you're calling—I'm fine." It's a big fat lie and everyone knows it, but she humors me with silence. Trying to convince her, I add, "I promise. I'm doing play dates, my kitchen is fully stocked, and I appreciate you calling, but I'm okay this year."

"Okay, just checking on you. You are doing better." Her words of encouragement are sincere. If she had said them a year ago, I would have laughed. On this date last year, I was a train wreck.

"Thanks, Lanie. I'll catch up with you later."

The sky is blue today. Billowy white clouds float by as if it is just another day, but it's not. Two years... It's been two years today since I found out Cade was gone. If one more person tells me *he's in a better place* I might just scream. I want him here with me, with our baby. I wanted to see his face when he held our son for the first time, but that life is gone.

I try to accept it, but today is harder than other days. Last year I cried all day. This year, I want to simply be grateful I had him in my life for so long. Some couples only have months. We had years.

I want to learn to be grateful, but resentment still lingers. I lost him too soon. At times like this, a friend stops by and I fall for it. I let them in, we chat for a bit and they'll show me a new manicure with some weird design on the tips or the Ombre in their hair. They talk about the things that were a part of my life before CJ, my sweet baby.

Now, I barely have time to breathe. I haven't been to a salon since before he was born, and nails—ha! Mine are cut short and nude. That's right. I've got naked nails.

When I get to the house, Lanie's already there. I should have known. After laying CJ down, I start picking up.

SECOND CHANCES

"Genny, sit. You're always running." I oblige and plop down on the couch next to her. God, my feet hurt. I sigh and slouch back, closing my eyes for half a second, when I hear CJ whimper over the baby monitor. Ugh. That was a short nap. I think he has some kind of radar that sends off alerts to his baby brain whenever I sit down. I moan and put my arm over my face. I didn't have time to pick up much and the sink is still full of dirty dishes. Some might be growing a new breed of penicillin. My mother would be horrified.

"I'll get him, sweetie. You sit." Lanie grins and bounds up the stairs like a poodle on crack, taking them two at a time. I think she lives on Pixie Stix and Coca-Cola. I would try that diet, but my yoga pants don't stretch that far.

I can hear her voice on the baby monitor. "Hello, little CJ, pookie poo. Who loves his Aunt Lanie? You do! That's right, you perfect little man." She makes cooing noises and kissie sounds.

I can hear her through the static and she knows it. "Speaking of great men, I met the nicest guy for Mommy the other day."

She's still talking in baby talk, so it sounds like she's hitting on my soon-to-be toddler.

Lanie goes on, chattering to CJ. "Really, CJ, you gotta tell Mama that this guy would be perfect for her! He's nice and tall and hot. Can you say hot? Hot. Hot!"

CJ mimics her but it comes out wrong. "Bah."

"Yes, I think so, too," she answers him. Their voices fade, her footfalls getting louder until she descends the staircase. CJ sees me and squirms, crying for me. I hold out my arms and she hands him over. I tuck the baby under my chin and kiss his chubby cheek.

"Why don't you come out with us tomorrow night? We can get dressed up," she wrinkles her nose as she glances over at my wrinkled, baby-barf covered t-shirt and black yoga pants, "and you can meet him!"

I immediately start shaking my head, and her face falls. "Lanie, I *can't*."

She blinks rapidly and presses her hand to her chest. "Oh, my god! How embarrassing. I was asking CJ, not you." She laughs and I swat her with the burp

SECOND CHANCES

cloth that was laying on the arm of the couch.

"Lanie, I'm just not ready yet." And I'm not. I still love my *husband*, and there's no escape from that. His rings are still on my finger. He might be gone, but in my mind I'm still married. Besides, I'm reminded of him every time I look at my little boy's face. He looks just like his father, right down to his blonde hair and brown eyes. I don't think he inherited anything from me at all and I'm glad. Losing Cade hasn't gotten easier, but having little Cade Junior—my precious baby, CJ—the only piece of his daddy that remains, makes things a little better.

Lanie squirms in her seat and tips her head at me. It's the sympathetic head tilt. It's usually a cue for me to run the other way, because whatever's coming out of her mouth next is going to suck monkeys. She clasps her hands under her chin and then lets the words fly, pleading. "Aw, honey, it's been two years! He wouldn't want you to be alone forever! Don't you want a father for CJ?"

Her eyes are begging me to give this guy a chance, but I won't, and the fact that she keeps pushing guy after guy at me makes me upset. She doesn't get it—I want to be alone, take care of my son, and raise him so he knows his father. Besides, I'm not looking to replace my Cade, I don't know how I'd ever love someone as much as I loved him. And, in the off chance that I could, I'd never be able to endure loss like this again. It nearly destroyed me. There were nights that were so long and horrific that I didn't think I'd see the next morning. If CJ wasn't here, I don't know what would have become of me.

"Lanie, I don't know why you keep trying to force me into this! It never works out well. The last guy you introduced me to," I use air quotes for the introduced part, "said, and I quote, 'I'm not looking for a relationship, I just want to have a good time. You up for that?' Gah, could you pick a bigger loser?" The baby stays nestled in the crook of my neck, his little fingers playing with the frizz of my hair.

Lanie makes a face. "Everyone needs to get laid once in a while."

SECOND CHANCES

Death stare. I do it without thinking and glare at her forehead, wishing I could give her more brains, or a nicer brain, a brain that stops meddling and accepts me the way I am—a broken mess. "Ixnay on getting laid in front of the baby!"

It's gotten to the point where I do everything possible *not* to go out with our friends. Going out had been fun before Cade died, but it's turned into a *get Genny to move on* exercise. Cade is a hard act to follow. He loved me. It's hard to describe, but I feel like we're still together, that he's still mine and I'm still his—even though he's gone. No other guy holds a candle to Cade, and no guy ever will. Their meddling makes me want to scream at times, even though I know they mean well. The thing is, I don't need a man and CJ doesn't need another daddy. He already has one. But they all get in on it, everyone picking a different guy for me to try out, pushing me into the arms of someone new.

"He doesn't know what I'm saying. Besides, it's not like it'll give him some sort of Oedipus complex to know his mom doesn't want to be alone for the rest of her life. Mommy needs to get some, Little Man." She smiles at CJ, like this is an acceptable conversation to have in front of my baby.

I yank him away and her smile turns to a frown. "God, Lanie, it feels like you want me to turn into the town whore and sew a red A on my chest."

"Yes, I do, but only if A is for 'available.'"

"CJ already has a father, Lanie, and today isn't a good day to push me." Glaring at her, I say firmly, "I think it's time for you to go."

I'm so over all the pushing and the pressure. I know they mean well, really, I do, but I'm just so *tired* of pretending. I'm tired of pretending to be happy, pretending to be ready. I don't think I'll ever be ready to let him go. How do you let go of the one person who knew everything about you, the good and the bad, and loved you anyway? I've had true love once, I don't want to go through the pain of losing someone else if I'm lucky enough to find love again. CJ is all I need.

SECOND CHANCES

"Gen, don't be like that! Gen, I…" Lanie's stammering gets cut off by a knock on the front door. Standing up, I ignore her apologies and scoot past her. Pulling open the door, I snap, "What?" before registering the guy standing in front of me on the porch.

"Uh, hi, Mrs. Prior," he says, rubbing a hand along the back of his neck and smiling sheepishly at me. "I just wanted to let you know that I mowed the yard, and I fixed the loose board in the back steps so you won't have to worry about falling with CJ in your arms." He smiles warmly at the baby on my hip and waves at him. CJ giggles once and buries his face in my shoulder. Daniel looks up at me. "I'll, uh, I'll see you next week?" The last is a question, and I'm sure he thinks I'm mad at him. Ooops.

I feel like a jerk for snapping. "Sorry, I didn't mean to snap at you! Thanks, Daniel," I attempt to sound friendly, even though I'm still fuming thanks to Lanie. "Please, call me Genevieve, okay? Mrs. Prior just makes me feel old." I smile at him, trying to make up for my earlier rudeness.

Daniel nods a goodbye and jogs down the steps to the *Clement Landscaping* truck sitting at the curb. With a sigh, I shut the door and turn back to face Lanie, who looks close to tears.

"Genny, I'm sorry. I just want you to be happy again." Her eyes are filled almost to over-flowing and me to forgive her.

I lean back against the door, CJ still in my arms, and stare at her. She has no idea, no one does. "Will you *please* let *me* decide when and *if* I'm ready to move on?" My voice isn't angry anymore, it's weary. I'm tired of having to explain this to everyone all the time. I'll move on when I'm ready, and not a minute before.

Moving away from the door and back toward the couch, I shift CJ and hold him close. At just over a year old, he's still more baby than toddler, and I love his sweet smell. It's nothing like Cade's, but still so precious to me. He reaches up to tug my messy ponytail, gripping the hair tight in his fist and babbling at me.

Lanie watches me sit on the floor to play with my little boy. When he starts to bang on one of his toys, I realize that this is

SECOND CHANCES

how I spend the majority of my time; at home, by myself, with CJ. Every so often, a friend or my mom comes over to try to get me outside the house, but they don't come as often as they have in the past. It's good in some ways, because they all think I should at least attempt to move on, to have a relationship with someone else. And, just like Lanie, they think I should find another father for CJ.

Every time I look at this healthy little boy, I see my husband. How am I supposed to move on when I love Cade just as much now as I did the day he deployed? How do I ask another man to share my heart with someone? I'll never stop loving Cade, and it seems unfair to start something with someone else, knowing that I can't give it my whole heart. Yes, sometimes I am lonely. Doing everything myself is hard, harder than I thought it would be, but I can manage on my own. Things will get easier as he gets older.

And then what, Gen? I ask myself. *He goes off to school and you sit alone? He won't be here forever.*

I shove the thought aside. That day is too far away to fathom. I'm lucky in some ways; Cade made sure that if something happened to him, I would be taken care of. There was enough insurance money to pay off the house and to allow me to live more than comfortably. Only my mother knows how much he left for us. I never knew he upped his policy. I've got more money than I could spend. Okay, I could probably spend all of it on this house. It's in such need of attention. It's so old and worn. Thankfully, I have Daniel to take care of any issues that come up, like the steps out back. The board warped and the edge lifted just enough to catch my toe while I was carrying in a bag of yard toys. Daniel saw me fall and immediately started working to fix the warped step.

Cade hired Daniel while he was still in high school, and he's been taking care of our lawn ever since. Since Cade's death, Daniel has been slowly taking on more responsibilities, helping with not only the yard, but also leaky faucets, broken drawers, stuck closet doors; I don't know what I would have done without his help over the past two years. Daniel quietly goes about his business, checking on things. Sometimes he seems intimidated by me, but he always smiles at CJ and talks to him.

"Are you ever going to speak to me again?" Lanie's voice is quiet, and I can tell she feels awful for pushing me, especially today out of all days.

It's hard to stay mad at her. Pinching the bridge of my nose in an attempt to ward off the headache I can feel forming behind my eyes, I shake my head. "Of course I'm going to talk to you again, but promise me something."

I get a face full of doe eyes. "Sure."

"Promise to stop butting in. When I'm ready to date, you'll be the first person to know."

"But, what if I find a great guy who would be perfect for you?"

"What if the moon falls on my head?"

"What if he doesn't mind and likes girls with big, flat heads?" I snort, trying not to laugh. She rolls her shoulders forward like a sulky teenager and groans. "I'm going to have to introduce you. There's just no other option! I mean, what are the odds that a guy would like a girl with a flat head like that? It's one in a billion. I'd hate for you to miss out on your second chance just because you didn't think you were ready." Her eyes are pleading with me, even as she smiles winningly. "And you know, if the moon does fall on your head we'll have to cover it with a hat or something. Does Macy's make hats that big? And you'd glow a bit, I suppose. People would notice your noggin was abnormally large, but some guys like that kind of thing, Gen. They've got some weird kinks going on."

I roll my eyes, knowing there's no way I'm going to stop her from trying to help, no matter how much I don't want her to. "Fine, whatever. But, no guilt tripping me into going on a blind date with anyone. No tricking me, either!" She grins, knowing she's winning and I point a finger at her. "I mean it, Lanie. No telling me we're going out for drinks when we're actually going on a double date. I know how you are."

"Promise!" she squeals, running over to hug me and squeezing me tight. "Oh, we are going to find you the *best* guy ever! I can't wait!"

SECOND CHANCES

"Ugh... Lanie," I groan when she lets me go, but I can't stop the smile that spreads across my face in reaction to the huge one on hers. She's bouncing up and down on the balls of her feet, her blonde hair flying everywhere, and clapping her hands. "You're such a dork," I tell her with a laugh.

She stops bouncing to put her hands on her hips. "That may be true, Genny, but I'm *your* dork." We both burst into giggles and I'm glad I have such good friends. Even if they do keep trying to find me a man when I'm not interested. I'll just have to make sure I don't fall for any tricks around her. She's a weasel when she wants to be.

Lanie spends the rest of the afternoon at my house, convincing me to join her, Maggie, and Erin, at a new club they found. As much as I think they are full of it, and against my better judgment, I agree to go along the following evening.

I spend the rest of this day snuggling with CJ. I mean to put him down to sleep in his room, but we end up snuggling in my bed, instead. I watch him sleep and pray to a God that ignores me, hoping Cade can hear my words.

*****

Lanie paws through my closet, pulling out dresses. "This!" She squeals excitedly.

"Yeah, no." My best friend pouts when I refuse to let her pick what I'm wearing, and she pouts even harder when she sees I plan to wear jeans, a t-shirt and sneakers for this night out.

"Genny! What are you doing? Please tell me you're not wearing mom clothes to a club! Are you?" Lanie looks horrified. She's fully dressed in her 'do me now' gear—a short, tight black dress and what she lovingly refers to as hooker heels. Her shoes are at least six-inches-high and I would break my neck if I even attempted to walk around in them. I'm much safer in sneakers. I've never really been a girly-girl, and I see no reason to start now.

After a fifteen-minute argument about what I'm wearing, I throw Lanie out of my room, refusing to let her comb through my closet again. She pulled out every single dress I own and the only pair of heels I own, insisting I wear anything except of jeans and sneakers. She exercised all her influence in convincing me to go out drinking, though. I'm not changing. She can forget it.

By the time we are all finally ready to leave, I'm the least dressed up person in our little foursome. I'm okay with that. While Erin and Lanie are out trolling for men, I have all the man I need at home. Mom and Daddy are babysitting for the evening and Maggie's hubby is driving us. It's her girl's night out for the month and she's planning on drinking – a lot.

Lanie leans in to whisper-shout in my ear, "He's only volunteering to drive because he's hoping he'll get lucky when they get home tonight."

Maggie yells at her, "Shut up! That's not true!" But I can see the grin on Luke's face in the mirror. He's totally hoping he's going to get lucky tonight.

Chapter 5

I can't believe I let Lanie talk me into this. I'm so out of place in the club. Lanie, Maggie and Erin are all on the dance floor, and even though they're in their early thirties, they're wearing short dresses and sky-high heels. Lanie divorced before Cade died, and Erin was engaged once, but it didn't work out. Maggie, on the other hand, got married two months after Cade and I did. She and Luke have been happily married ever since.

I have no idea why I even agreed to come here. I'm not looking for a man and, now that I'm here, I'd much rather be at home, playing with my son. Instead, I'm

SECOND CHANCES

sitting here wearing jeans and a t-shirt in a club where everyone else is dressed up. I stick out like a nun in a whorehouse. Every other woman here is glittering and showing off skin. Bare midriffs, shoulders, backs, and high-cut skirts leave little to the imagination. I tip my head sideways and check out some other girl's ass. I think I can see the bottom of her butt. I blink twice and shake my head. I never dressed like that. Geeze, she might as well prance through the place naked.

Watching my friends shake their asses on the dance floor is actually pretty funny. All three of them have had about four times more alcohol than I have—and I've only had one cocktail. I'm such a lightweight that drinking doesn't benefit me at all. I'm also not the happiest drunk, especially these days. I'd end up crying into my drink and gushing about Cade.

"Hi there, pretty lady." The voice comes from my left, and when I turn around, there's a random guy who looks to be at least five years older than me. He's wearing a suit that doesn't fit him very well and his eyes are glazed with the amount of alcohol he's consumed. The smell of beer is coming off him in waves, making me want to gag. Don Juan, he is not.

Forcing a smile onto my face, I eek out a, "Hi," and turn back to my drink. I'm hoping against hope that he takes the hint, realizes I'm not into him and moves on to greener, or at least drunker, pastures.

"What's a pretty girl like you doing sitting here all by herself?" He's leering at me now, clearly thinking he's an amazing conversationalist.

I groan inwardly, glad I wore my wedding rings tonight. They may be the only things that save me from drunken idiots with awful pick up lines. "Sorry, waiting for my husband," I tell him, flashing my rings in his face.

Unfortunately, my wedding rings don't deter him at all. He sways drunkenly toward me, his beer breath is overpowering. "Well, I guess your husband's missing out tonight," he slurs, "because I just found the prettiest girl in the room."

'Pretty' seems to be his go-to word to make a girl swoon. It's hard to believe this guy doesn't have panties dropping all around the bar. But, what *really* pisses me off is that he has no respect for wedding vows. I sneak a glance at his left hand, relieved to see no ring or tan line suggesting that he usually wears one. Not that it proves anything, but hopefully he's not out cheating on a wife tonight.

"Okay," I say, trying to laugh about the situation. I don't want to hurt his feelings, not really, but I'm seriously not interested. "Uh, look. I'm sure you're a great guy—but I have a husband and I'm really not looking for anyone else. Have a good night, alright?" I move to step around him, but his hand closes tight around my upper arm. His grip is hard enough to leave a mark, and worry creeps into me.

Drunk Guy's eyes turn hard as he watches me. "Where do you think you're going? We were just getting to know each other." Maybe it's the amount of alcohol he's had tonight, but he isn't taking the hint. As much as I don't want to be mean to someone, anxiety is eating away at my ability to keep up social pleasantries. Honestly, I'm not even sure an outright, cold, rejection is going to work, but I have to try.

I open my mouth to tell him how much I'm not interested when a familiar deep voice says, "Hey, baby. I was wondering where you were." I sigh in relief, grateful I won't have to make a scene. Daniel's arm goes around my shoulder and he uses his free hand to peel Drunk Guy's from my arm.

"Ow! What the fuck, man? We were just talking." The drunk seems extremely confused about this turn of events. He stares at his arm and then up at Daniel.

Eager to get away from him and not wanting the lawn boy to break my cover, I shout, "Remember that husband I mentioned?" Curling deeper into Daniel's embrace, I place a hand on his very hard stomach, "Well, this is him."

Drunk Guy looks dejected, and just stares at us without another word. Daniel steers me away and over to a hallway that's pretty empty and a whole lot quieter than the rest of the club.

"What was that about?" He's looking down at me, and once again I'm reminded of just how much he's grown up in the past few years. He had been a wiry kid when I first met him. Now he's filled out, all muscle, with broad shoulders, dark hair, and blue eyes. Stubble lines the jaw of his tan face. He should wear sunscreen. I bet he doesn't.

I shrug and look over my shoulder, glad to be rid of the guy. "Just some drunk who was looking to get lucky. Why he would try me out of all the women here is beyond me." I smirk. "He must have been drunker than he looked."

"Why wouldn't he try with you?" Daniel cocks his head to the side, studying me intently.

I feel self-conscious under his appraisal and wave away his question. "Ha, yeah. I don't think so."

"No," he says firmly. "I really want to know. You're beautiful, Mrs. Prior, why wouldn't he be interested in you?"

Laughingly, I answer, "Are you serious?" He narrows his eyes at me, but doesn't reply. "Have you *seen* some of the women in here tonight? They're wearing dresses that don't leave anything to the imagination, complete with totally doable fuck-me heels." My voice turns mocking as I present myself like a game-show prize. "Meanwhile, behind door B is Genevieve, wearing jeans and a t-shirt, complete with a stain over the left boob. Sexy, I know." I laugh.

But Daniel shakes his head and looks at his hands. After a moment, he looks up at me from under dark lashes. "You don't see yourself very clearly do you? It's not your clothes that make you beautiful." I stare blankly at him, confused. "Mrs. Prior, uh, Genevieve, you're more beautiful than any other woman in here tonight. He'd be a fool to pick one of them over you."

I have no words.

When I heard his voice earlier, all I felt was relief. I never expected to hear anything like this come out of his mouth! He's too nice, and it must be obvious how rough of a night I've been having. Tucking a piece of hair behind my ear, I confess, "You don't have to try to make me feel better, Daniel. I know exactly what I look like, and there are way prettier women in here than me. Besides, you're, what, twenty-one? Surely there's a girl here your age you'd prefer to me."

His eyes narrow and I know I crossed a line. I'm not sure what line I crossed, but his reaction is instant.

"I'm going to pretend you didn't say any of that," he says angrily, "and, for the record, I'm twenty-two. I'd also pick spending time with you over a hook up with *a woman my own age* any night of the week and I'll prove it to you." He takes my hand and drags me toward the dance floor.

I know he's spent a lot of time at my house, but he's obviously not spent enough time there to see what me dancing looks like. It's not pretty... not at all. I'm pretty sure I was born without the rhythm gene. Granted, I'm sure it will be great entertainment for spectators. I dig my feet in, trying to find traction on the floor, saying, "But, Daniel, I don't dance," again and again isn't working. He doesn't release my hand and, for some idiotic reason, I let him pull me toward the dance floor. I'm not sure if he's not hearing me or if he's just choosing not to listen. Either way, this isn't a good thing.

Daniel takes us straight to the middle of the floor, where the women I thought he'd prefer close in around us. Regardless, he doesn't look at anyone but me, and my stomach flips as he smiles at me. He turns me around so that my back is against his front and puts his hands on my hips. The heat of his body burns me everywhere it touches and I forget why I didn't want to come out here.

The song that's playing is unfamiliar, but has a heavy baseline. Daniel's hands on my hips start moving me in time with the beat, keeping his hips against mine. Shocked that I'm actually moving to the music, even though I know it's his talent not mine, I close my eyes and enjoy the ride. It's been a long time since I've been touched by someone that wasn't one of my parents, Lanie, Maggie or Erin - and it's been over two years since I was touched by a man I'm not related to in some way.

We stay out on the dance floor for two more songs. The second song we dance to is fast, with another bass beat, but the third song is slower. The girl singing the song is crooning about how much she adores a guy.

SECOND CHANCES

It's something I've heard before, but I have no idea who's singing it.

Daniel turns me to face him, taking my hands and wrapping them around his neck so that I'm holding onto him. He pulls me close, wrapping his own arms around my waist and moving us to the music. Our eyes are locked together, unable to look away and I feel things that are definitely familiar, but that I haven't felt for a long time.

We stay like that for the rest of the song, barely moving back and forth although, every movement we make brushes our bodies together in very nice ways. By the time the song ends, I'm trembling, unable to look away from the heat in Daniel's eyes. I know this is dangerous and I need to go, but I'm drawn to him. We watch each other, lost in a trance. I'm hyperaware of his hands on my skin and the way my breath catches in my throat. I'm also aware that I don't want this moment to end. The world around us fades away and we stay like that, close enough to kiss. His eyes drift over my face and dip to my lips before returning to my eyes.

The desire to trace my finger over his jaw shoots through me and, as I lift my hand to do so, a voice rings out. "Hey Chica!" Lanie's voice is extra loud in my ear and I jump, ripping myself right out of his arms and abandoning the plan to touch his cheek. I feel instantly bereft, missing his touch, which is beyond silly. I've known him for years, but not like this. This connection between us, whatever I just felt, can't be there. He's the kid next door, for crying out loud! I breathe in once, trying to blow off the crazy thoughts running through my imagination. He's just being sweet. I'm sure he only wanted to make me feel better after my encounter with Drunk Guy. It was a pity dance, that's all.

"Are you ready to go? Luke is here to get us." Lanie is smirking.

I can see Daniel's questioning gaze and I'm quick to explain, "Luke is Maggie's husband. He's our driver tonight." His face clears as he leans down to brush a kiss against my cheek.

"Thanks for the dances, Genevieve." He leans closer to whisper in my ear, "I wish we could have danced longer." My

SECOND CHANCES

stomach flips when he speaks. He can't be serious, can he? I glance back at him, astonished, as he inclines his head in polite goodbye to Lanie, Erin and Maggie, and then disappears in the crowd.

Lanie gives me a strange look, "What was that about, Genny?"

"Nothing," I say, quickly. "Daniel just saved me from a very hands-on drunk and we danced for a few songs to keep the guy away. No big deal." The lie rolls off my tongue quickly and falls to the ground with a thump. It shouldn't be a big deal and I doubt it was to him. "He was just being sweet, that's all."

Erin snorts, "It sure looked like a big deal. I think that boy has a crush on you, Genny!" My face flames at her words.

"He does not!" I snap, defending him. "Come on, you guys. It was just harmless dancing. And, besides, didn't you say Luke is here? We shouldn't keep him waiting. He was nice enough to let Maggie out to play." Maggie sticks her tongue out at me and we all laugh.

This club thing seemed like a very bad idea when we got here. It's funny how a couple of dances with Daniel completely changed my perspective. I felt more like the girl I had been, the formerly fun Genny, tonight than I have in a long, long time. He's a sweet kid.

As we file out the door, I feel eyes on my back and look around. I see Daniel across the room, standing alone and watching me with eyes that are just as heated now, as they were when we were dancing earlier. A shiver snakes down my spine. I have to be imagining it, because there's no way he'd be into me. Not like that. Confused, I smile and mouth *thank you*, at him, before walking out of the club with my friends. I wonder what's going to happen when he comes over to the house next time, if he'll act the way he always does. My bet is that he'll pretend this never happened. Alcohol does weird things to people. It's only after I make that excuse for his behavior, that I realize I didn't smell a drop of liquor on him.

Chapter 6

CJ has been sick for almost a week now, and I'm losing my mind. It's breaking my heart because he won't stop crying, and I can't find a way to comfort him. He spits out the medicine his doctor gave me and we're both miserable. I haven't slept in days. CJ is constantly unhappy and, the few times he's dozed off from exhaustion, I've been too paranoid to sleep. What if he's tangled in his blankets and can't breathe? What if he has SIDs? What if a plastic bag floats into the room and lands on his head? Too many morbid thoughts flash through my mind. I'm not exactly stable when CJ isn't sick. The stress of his high temperature has me beside myself.

I'm strong, I can do this. God won't give me more than I can handle. I chant the phrase over and over, but it offers no comfort. I feel like God abandoned me years ago. We don't talk anymore. I no longer believe in prayers or miracles. Nothing will change my mind, not after so many pleading prayers fell on deaf ears. God ignored me when I needed him most. I asked Him to spare my husband. I begged. I pleaded. I told Him that I'd do anything, but nothing changed. Cade is gone and I'm alone, and I really miss him at times like this.

I've taken my poor baby back and forth to the pediatrician three times in the past few days, trying to help him feel better. First, it was an ear infection, and not just an ear infection, but a *double* ear infection—his second one this month. The doctor said that if he keeps getting them, they'll have to put tubes in his ears. It's completely routine, but putting my son to sleep for surgery at his age is not something I want to do. I don't know how much of my fear is from the surgery, or from the thought of

SECOND CHANCES

losing him in a freak complication. Either way, I know I couldn't bear it. I'm not strong enough to lose anyone else.

The second time I took CJ to the doctor, the ear infection was doing better, but the antibiotics caused stomach problems. We went through diapers like they were nothing. Diapers are expensive, but that wasn't the worst part—CJ was still crying. His stomach hurt and he didn't want anything except milk, which wouldn't stay in him. The doctor suggested giving him rice cereal. CJ disagreed and fervently let me know that he was not happy.

The third time, we were back because CJ stopped eating entirely. The crying was worse. I couldn't tell what was wrong, but soon found out that the white spots in his mouth weren't uneaten food. They were Thrush, which is apparently very painful—which was why he wouldn't eat and continued to cry. I'd never seen thrush, or ever heard of it. If I'd known, I could have eased his pain sooner, but I didn't know. I'm so scared that I'm going to make a horrible mistake, and I'm so tired. My body is screaming at me to stop, to lie down, but I can't.

This week has rattled me to the core. It doesn't help that my mom keeps calling, every hour on the hour, to check on CJ. Rationally, I know she's just as worried as I am. Emotionally, I feel as though I should be waiting for Child Protective Services to show up and take him away from me. What kind of mother can't comfort her child?

CJ is tugging his ear and crying. His little face is scrunched up as he wails. I'm about to lose it. I can't stand to hear him hurting. I try again with the medicine, but he fights me, smacking at the dropper and blocking it with his tongue.

"Come on, Baby. It'll make you feel better. I promise. Mommy wouldn't make you do it if it didn't help. Come on Little Man, just a little bit." I have him lying on the couch with his arms pinned. I manage to get the dropper between his teeth, which makes him wail. I squirt the medicine in and it goes straight down his throat, choking him. His big brown eyes look at me like I'm a monster as he gags. But, the medicine finally goes down his throat.

SECOND CHANCES

I scoop him up in my arms, even though he pushes me away, and start crying right along with him. I'd been so determined to prove to my parents, my friends, and everyone else that I could do this on my own. It seemed like the only way to get them off my back about remarrying. Now, I'm sitting on the couch, in the middle of a breakdown, clutching my baby and sobbing uncontrollably. When there's a knock on the door, I simply ignore it.

"Genevieve?" a male voice comes from behind me and I jump, swiveling around to see who's there. Standing in the doorway, looking at me sheepishly, is Daniel. He looks around the room and I'm mortified. The house is a mess. The kitchen smells and I haven't taken out the garbage in two days. Add in the stuff growing in the sink and I can't hide my horror.

Standing, I try to block the worst of the damage with my body, but nothing hides the smell. "Uh, hi Daniel. Did you need something?" I'm self-conscious at the thought of someone seeing me this way. Instantly aware of the fact that I haven't showered in two days, I'm still wearing the clothes I put on yesterday and my unwashed hair is falling out of the ponytail holder. I'm as messy and smelly as the house. Running a hand over my head in an attempt to somewhat restore order to my dark hair, I know I'm blushing furiously as Daniel looks on, a concerned frown on his face.

He points back towards the door when he says, "I heard the baby crying earlier and wanted to make sure everything was alright. Is he okay?"

I sniffle and wipe away the tears, trying to act like it's nothing. "CJ's been sick for a few days and I can't seem to do anything to make him feel better." My voice cracks on the last word and I start to suck in tiny, rapid breaths like I'm going to burst into tears again. I turn away, wondering why I'm telling him this, why I'm letting him know just how awful I am as a mother. I notice CJ has finally stopped bawling and lay my sweet boy down in his playpen. The weight of CJ's absence feels too heavy, and my hands shoot up, nervously pulling on and smoothing my hair.

SECOND CHANCES

That's when Daniel steps around me and catches my eye. His expression is sympathetic, not full of the judgment I expect. He gently catches my hands and holds them in his own.

"Genevieve," he says softly, "is there someone you can call to watch him for a little while, so you can sleep?" The idea of sleep sounds so good. I think of my mother, but being as worried as I am, she'd spend the entire time she was here *helping* me by suggesting more things that could go wrong.

I shake my head frantically, jerking my hands out of his. "No, I don't want to call anyone. I can't. I can do this by myself. I have to. It's just hard." My voice is rising, and I know I must sound hysterical.

"Everyone thinks they understand, but they can't. They have no clue, none at all. There are no breaks. There's no one to tell when CJ does something cute or silly. There's no one to share with, the good or the bad.

"He must hate me, Daniel. I've been pinning him down to force-feed him his medicine. It breaks my heart, but I don't know how else to do it. He must hate me. When he pushes me away, I die inside. When a kid is mad at one parent, they're supposed to be able to run to the other – but CJ has no one to run to." My voice is so screechy by the time I finish that I sound mental. I just dumped my heart out on the lawn boy. What the hell is wrong with me? I clutch my face and shove away the tears. I just want someone to know that I'm trying. I'm trying to be both mommy and daddy, and on days like today I feel like I'm failing miserably. Choking back sobs, I try to hold myself together. The past few days have taken their toll and I'm coming apart at the seams.

"Hey now, it's okay. CJ needs you as much as you need him. You guys will be fine, you've just hit a rough patch." Daniel wipes the tears from my cheeks and tips his head to the side. He holds on a beat too long, watching me too closely, before releasing me. His gaze drops and when they flick back up he seems like he's made a decision. "Listen, if you won't let me call anyone, why don't you let me watch him for a little while? You can get a nap in, and you'll feel better."

The auto-responder in my brain speaks for me. "No, I can't ask you to do that." I glance at Daniel and then down at the baby.

"If you don't take care of yourself, you won't be able to take care of CJ and he needs you."

Suddenly nervous, I start to stammer, "I can't. It's okay, Daniel. Besides, I'm sure you have plenty of things to do." I'm embarrassed that he's seen even this much of the house, and I shudder to think what he'll see if he ventures any further inside.

He grins and folds his tanned arms over his muscular chest. "I'm not leaving."

"Yes, you are. I'm fine now. See?" I flash him a fake smile that's all teeth.

He laughs. "You hate asking for help. I get that, believe me, I get that—but there are times when you need it and you have no choice in the matter. Today, my friend, you are getting help from Dan the lawn man.. End of story."

I'm tempted. I'm so tempted, but he hasn't sold me yet. I can't leave him alone with CJ. "Do you even know *how* to take care of a baby?"

"Stop," he says commandingly, and my eyes fly up to meet his. Daniel puts a hand on my back, gently pushing me towards the stairs. "Go, Genevieve. Take a nap, get some real rest. And yes, I know how to take care of a baby. I have a little sister. I've got this, I promise." Without another word, he turns and holds out his arms for CJ. My son, the little merciful traitor, lifts his hands up and Daniel takes him from the playpen and balances him on his hip. "Go on, Genevieve. We're good here." They head to the kitchen, chattering softly.

Defeated, I give in. Heading up the stairs, I try to decide if I'd rather take a shower or a nap. The two-day scent makes me drag my lead-filled legs to the bathroom. It's the first time in I'm not sure how long that I've been able to wash up without worrying about CJ being alone in the house. While I undress, I can hear Daniel talking to CJ through the baby monitor.

"Hey, buddy," he says, his voice low and soothing, much like it was earlier when

SECOND CHANCES

he was talking to me. CJ was still whimpering when I went upstairs. Now I can hear his little hiccup breaths which slow and finally stop, as Daniel talks to him. "You are running your mama ragged, do you know that? She hates that you aren't feeling good, did you know that? Your mama loves you so much. She'd do anything for you. You're a lucky man to have a lady like that—very lucky."

He's talking to CJ like he's much older than he is, and I have to cover my mouth to hide the giggles that are bubbling up inside me. Boy, I really am sleep deprived if listening to him talk to my son has me so close to hysterics. Instead of getting into the shower, I listen intently to their conversation, my heart melting at the things he's saying.

"Poor guy, you've had it pretty rough this week, huh? I don't know exactly what's been bothering you, but I know your mom's looked more upset each time I've seen her. Today, when I came up the steps to let her know I was leaving, I could hear her crying. I bet you could tell she was sad, huh? I know it made me want to comfort her, so I'm sure you wanted to too. Is that why you were crying, buddy? You wanted to make your mom feel better, but you were stuck being sick? It sucks, doesn't it? Wanting to make someone feel better but not being able to is horrible, right?"

Daniel's voice fades as they leave CJ's room, and I find myself wishing he'd taken the monitor with him so I could continue to listen in. In the few interactions we've had, Daniel's the only one who hasn't judged me. He's never given me his opinion though, so I don't really know what he thinks I should be doing.

Wondering about his motives and what he really wants, I finally get in the shower, practically moaning—okay, maybe there wasn't any practically about it—at the feel of the hot water sluicing over my body. I take my time washing my hair and putting conditioner in, something I hardly ever use because it takes extra time, and massage my scalp. I also take my time running the loofa over my skin, slowing when I run my hand over my scarred stomach. CJ was such a big baby. Some women get away with a few lines, but my skin looks like a roadmap. I tried coconut oil and stretch mark cream, but nothing made them fade. When I was Daniel's age, my stomach was flat and my skin was smooth and supple. I trace one of the scars with the pad of my finger, watching the soap run down my mommy thighs.

The other night was weird, dancing with him like that. I think about it as I slather soap everywhere, breathing deeply in my attempt to activate the stress relief body wash. It doesn't work all that well for me. Maybe I'm supposed to eat it to achieve the full effect. Mommies must be the reason there are so many silly warnings on consumer products.

I smile as my thoughts linger back to dancing with Daniel. I liked the way he held me, how safe I felt in his arms. At the end of the day, life is about relationships and being alone sucks. It was nice to have someone stick up for me and not try to pry their way into my thoughts. I giggle to myself. Maybe he has a crush on me. I know I'm seriously over-tired because I'm totally over analyzing this. He's just really sweet, that's all.

But, it didn't go unnoticed that he said we were friends. I never thought of him that way, but I'm glad he said it. I'd help him in a second, I know I would. He's just been around so long that I never noticed him. Life's weird like that. I didn't notice how much he's grown up until the other night. I still saw him as the high school kid that Cade hired, all wiry and awkward. But he's not that boy anymore. We've both changed, for better or worse. My head is tipped so I'm leaning against the tile, half asleep. If I slip and Daniel has to come pick me up, I'll die. I've suffered enough embarrassment for one day. He could tell all his friends he helped some old lady out of the shower.

I look down at my breasts as I step out of the shower and pat dry. They're no longer as firm as they once were, and they've lost some of their perky youthfulness. Babies make everything point south and round out. I never really thought about what CJ did to my body. Cade's gone, and I haven't been trying to impress anyone. But the thoughts linger as my

SECOND CHANCES

fingers press against the slope of my chest, and for a second I miss my old body.

Where are these thoughts coming from? This isn't like me! I don't linger on things that will never be. So, why the sudden upset that my body has become a little softer and my skin isn't as silky anymore? The marks across my stomach, and the smaller ones on the sides of my breasts, came with the best present in the world—CJ.

I brush aside my wishful thoughts as the random musings of an overtired mommy. I crawl into bed and sink into the pillows. My eyes close and every thought flutters from my mind. Sleep finds me swiftly and carries me away.

Chapter 7

When I wake a few hours later, the first thing I notice is that it's pitch black in my bedroom. Jumping up, I start to panic because I don't hear any noise coming from CJ's baby monitor before remembering Daniel is here. Once I realize that the two of them are probably downstairs, I relax. Placing a hand over my heart, I wait for my breath to slow and my heartbeat to get back to normal before heading for the stairs.

As I walk back down, I can hear Daniel murmuring and CJ's happy laughter in return. Slowing my steps, I enjoy the silence that's been absent the past few days, and the fact that the house doesn't feel empty.

SECOND CHANCES

When I reach the living room, I come to a complete stop, shocked at what I see. The toys that were all over the floor are gone, back in the toy box next to the couch, the clothes that were half-folded are now folded neatly in the basket on the chair, and the floor has been freshly swept and mopped.

I can't believe it. He cleaned my house. Shocked, I stand there turning slowly, taking it all in. Holy shit. The place is cleaner than when I do it. I pinch my arm to make sure I'm awake. This is unreal. Then it hits me, the smell. It's not the noxious fumes of a neglected kitchen. Oh my God, is that bread?

Daniel's voice comes from the kitchen. My stomach is rumbling from the smell of the food wafting through the room and it draws me in. I stand in the doorway of the kitchen, in awe, again. Not only did he clean up the living room, he cleaned the kitchen too. The pots that were on the stove are gone, the surface sparkling. The sink is empty and the counters have been wiped down.

CJ is sitting in his highchair with Daniel sitting in front of him. He's making train sounds as the spoon inches closer to CJ's mouth. My adorable boy is kicking his legs happily, a goofy smile on his face, as he tries to grab the spoon out of Daniel's hand. Daniel is quick to move though, chuckling at the frown that flits across my son's face. When I start to walk into the room, CJ's eyes meet mine and his smile widens. He's obviously feeling better.

"Mama mama mamamamama," he babbles, earning a smile from me and a laugh from Daniel.

Noticing that CJ's attention has moved away from him, Daniel turns, a smile on his face. "Hey, Genevieve. Did you have a good nap? I think this little guy missed you. You seem like you feel better. Did you sleep well?"

All I can do is nod.

Every time he calls me by my full name, my chest squeezes. Cade was the only person to ever call me anything but Gen or Genny. He told me once that my name was beautiful and he rarely called me anything else. He always said that Gen was okay, but a beautiful girl like me should be called Genevieve. At the time, the thought made my knees weak, but now... now being called Genevieve just makes me weepy. I have to clear my throat before I speak. "Yes, I did. Thank you so much for cleaning up." My face heats, "You really didn't have to do that."

Daniel shrugs, "It was nothing. I'm glad I could help out." He turns back to the baby, continuing to feed him as he says, "There's chili on the stove if you're hungry, and some bread. We like to dip, don't we CJ? Mmmmm, sauce." He smiles at the baby and they both dip a piece of bread into the baby's food and take a bite. I blink. It's adorable, and gross. Daniel ate mashed peas on a chunk of bread to make CJ smile. Daniel looks over at me. "He wanted my chili, but I got him to settle for the bread. He's down with it as long as we dip together. Right, little man?" CJ giggles and bobs his head.

An unidentified emotion floods through my body, head to toe. It feels like admiration and something else. I can't stop staring at them, at the way they sit and smile at each other. Oh my God, it's the sweetest thing I've ever seen.

Daniel glances over at me. "Did I do something wrong?"

I blink and shake my head so frantically that it might fall off my shoulders. Holding up my hands, I say, "No! God, no. You did everything right. No one's been this kind to me in a really long time. I don't know what to say."

His blue gaze is locked with mine. For a moment we stay like that, and something lightens in my chest. He finally drops his gaze and tips his head toward the pot of chili. "Then don't say anything. Besides, we had fun, didn't we CJ?"

I grab a bowl and sit at the table across from Daniel and the baby. As I eat, I watch them interact, and I'm relieved to see that Daniel does know what he's doing. He's patient, never getting upset when CJ spits his food out and it gets on his shirt or hands. Periodically, they pick up their bread and scream 'dunk' like it's a war cry before munching, or in CJ's case slobbering, on the bread.

SECOND CHANCES

When I realize that Daniel isn't eating anything else, I ask, "Have you eaten?"

Daniel shakes his head, "No, I'll get something in a few minutes, as soon as CJ is cleaned up."

"No, I can clean him up. You need to eat something. You were in the yard all day and then did all this. I bet you haven't sat down for a second. Let me get you a bowl." I start to walk past him, back to the stove, but he grabs my arm, stopping me in my tracks.

"It's okay, really. I'm good. Let me take care of you guys, just this once, okay? I see how hard you work to make sure you're doing everything right, and you need to take care of yourself too. It's not going to do CJ any good if you get sick too."

I'm sure he doesn't mean for them to, but his words make me feel self-conscious. My heart twists in my chest and suddenly I'm aware of the fact that while I'm much more put together than I was when he walked in earlier, I'm still feeling frumpy with my yoga pants and t-shirt.

I look down, and it takes more effort than you'd think to move my eyes away from his sincere gaze, but I manage. Making a conscious effort to keep the sudden tears at bay, I slip out of his grasp and take the dirty dishes from supper to the sink.

I'm standing, scrubbing the bowl and spoon I used with much more force than necessary, when I feel him come up behind me. I can feel the heat of his body at my back, and I stiffen, unsure what he's doing. His fingers gently brush my hair away from my face, and back over my shoulder, causing me to shudder involuntarily.

"What just happened?" The concern in Daniel's voice is evident.

I squeeze my eyes shut, my grip on the bowl in my hand tightening, and say nothing at first. When I continue to stand there with my eyes closed, I feel his hands wrap around mine, gently removing the bowl and laying it in the sink. Then, he turns me to face him, putting a finger under my chin and tipping my head up so that I have no choice but to look at him when I finally glance up.

His eyes are dark blue, the color of the sky at dusk and the total opposite of Cade's warm brown ones. I feel vulnerable like this. Something happens when Daniel studies me intently, his eyes moving back and forth between mine. It's like he can see through me and I don't like it. I try to squirm away.

"Did I do something?" he asks softly, looking genuinely perplexed.

"No."

"Then what happened?"

"I don't know." I stand there, my heart pounding hard, as the truth spills over my lips. I really have no idea, but his words cut me. I don't know why and I don't understand.

His eyes flick back and forth between mine. "I think you do."

"I just..." I can't say it. The feeling finally forms into words and I stop speaking. I can't tell him.

Daniel leans in closer. He's a breath away, making my heart slap into my ribs. "You just?" He prompts me, lingering so close that I can feel the heat coming off his body.

I try to step back, and I bump into the counter. There's no where to run, but I want to get away. I don't like the things that are stirring within me. What does it mean? It can't be what it feels like. The way my skin tingles when he's near, the way I drink him in like I'm dying of thirst, the way his voice soothes me and excites me at the same time. I suck in a jagged breath and try to look down, but his hand is on my chin. I take it in mine and hold onto it so I don't have to maintain the eye contact. My touch startles him and we both look at our hands, and the way I slowly slide mine over his.

I swallow hard and say, "I just haven't had anyone talk to me like that in a long time. That's all." I'm thinking about Cade, and he knows it. It was the tone Daniel used. I'm not always an easy woman to deal with. I can be opinionated and I like to do things my way. I'll also run myself into the ground. Cade was the only person that ever tried to stop me. He always put me first and he told me when I was being stupid. Accepting help has always been one of my weaknesses because—in my mind—it means I'm weak.

As if he can read my mind, he says, "You're made of strong stuff, but that doesn't mean you have to do everything alone." He raises a single brow at me. "This can be our little secret if you want to continue being super woman, saving the world all by yourself. I won't tell anyone that you joined the top-secret-super-justice-alliance if you don't."

His words make me smile softly, a real smile. "I think you're mixing DC and Marvel a little bit there."

His jaw drops. "And she knows comics? Be still my heart."

"And he knows poetry?" I smile shyly, looking at my feet and then back into his eyes.

"We're a couple of—" his voice trails off and he shakes his head, grinning. An alarm goes off. It sounds like it's coming from his pants.

"That's a strange place to keep the Batphone." I blush after I realize what I've said.

He laughs and then looks down at the screen. The smile falls off his lips. "Shit," he mutters, his brow furrowed.

"What is it?"

"Nothing." He's lying, but I don't pry. "I didn't realize it was getting so late. Sorry, Genevieve, I should get going, I have an early class tomorrow." He grins sheepishly at me, before picking his truck keys up off the counter and leaning in to kiss my cheek lightly. "I'll see you tomorrow, okay?"

I nod dumbly as he walks out of the room, stopping to ruffle CJ's hair and say, "See you tomorrow, buddy."

The door shuts and the sound is deafening in my now quiet house. I pick up the baby and pad to the door. Turning the lock, and then collapsing with my back against it, I stare into space. What am I going to do? The feelings I'm having are foreign. I haven't had anything like them in years, and I'm terrified. I can't feel these kinds of things for him.

My heart is racing, and my palms are sweating. At the same time, the guy can make me smile and flirt! Me, flirting? I thought that part of me broke. Flirting's okay, right? It doesn't mean anything – and it's a helluva lot of fun. I can flirt and he can flirt back. It doesn't mean that there's anything there. It's just fun, that's all. And, it makes me happy. He's the only thing that's actually made me happy in years—Dan the lawn man..

I close my eyes. He's over ten years younger than me. What is that going to look like? Even if we just hang out, what will people think? The age gap is huge. He's in college and I'm a widow. It won't look right. Actually, it'll look very wrong.

CJ begins babbling and I smile down at him. I'm certain that he's telling me about all the fun he had today with Daniel. Taking him upstairs, I settle him in the bed with me after cleaning up his messy face.

I know letting the baby sleep with me is a bad precedent to set, but I need the comfort of having him close to me tonight. It doesn't take long for CJ to fall to sleep, but it takes longer for me, and not just because of the nap I had earlier. I can't shut my mind off, the possibilities and consequences of spending time with Daniel are running through my head.

What if? What if? What if? A million scenarios fly through my mind and none of them end well. I need a friend right now. He's just a friend. Everyone else can suck it if they don't like how young he is. Yeah, I'm all bluster in my bed with my baby asleep next to me, but if my mom found out—she'd have a stroke and I'd be a blabbering idiot.

I'm up until the early hours of the morning before finally succumbing to my exhaustion.

Chapter 8

"Genny Prior, you are never going to find a father for CJ if you don't start dressing like someone who knows the value of a shower." My mom's scolding tone irks the hell out of me, but I can't bring myself to fight back. I suppose that's what she's looking for, some signs of life under this dreary façade and oversized shirt.

Of course she looks pristine in her standard Grandma outfit, complete with polyester pants and blouse. Her hair is set, properly curled and colored with light gold highlights around her face. Bright red and gold earrings hang dangling by her cheek.

I stare idly at the room around me. In my mother's house, everything is clean and polished. There is a place for everything and everything is in its place. In my house there is a place for everything, yet nothing is in it. It's like a toddler tornado blew through the house—toys litter the rug, baskets of supplies are tipped over. This morning I removed one of his socks from a picture frame hanging on the wall and a foam football from the toilet. I have bigger things to worry about than man shopping. Why can't she see that?

Rubbing my hands over my face, I sigh, "Give it a rest, mom, please? I swear to you I do take showers." Then quietly add, "almost every day," as I bend over to pick up a toy. I toss it in the basket and say for the bazillionth time. "I love you dearly, but I'm not man shopping. As it is, the pickings are slim. What if I pick one out and he's the wrong size? They don't take returns. I can't get stuck with a man that doesn't fit right. A frumpy relationship would really mess with CJ, Ma." She cringes. I'm not sure if it's my analogy or the use of 'Ma,' like she's the stereotypical meddlesome mother from a

SECOND CHANCES

TV sitcom. "And, in case you didn't notice, I'm a fully capable thirty-three-year-old woman. In fact, I'm a thirty-three-year-old woman today!"

She sits on her pristine couch, next to me. "Yes, yes, we know, Gen. If you'll recall, I gave birth to you, so of course I know how old you are. I'm just trying to make you see," she pauses, scrunches her nose and gesturing to my baggy t-shirt, yoga pants and the messy knot of hair on the top of my head, "that it's time to get going again."

One side of my mouth quirks up, "I don't want to get going with anyone."

She hands me a present. Inwardly, I groan because I already know what it is. "Happy birthday, honey. I thought this would start you off nicely."

She starts to lecture me further, but my father cuts her off. "Leave her alone, Gail."

"It's just a present. There's nothing wrong with doting on my daughter. Open it, dear."

I tear away the pretty pink paper and open the box. Black fabric lines the inside, corner to corner. I can't tell what it is, except that it has a deep V-neck. Mom pulls the garment out of the box and holds it up. She's beaming, and my jaw drops. It's a little black dress. A very sexy little nothing of a dress. "You bought me hooker clothes? Mom! What am I supposed to do with this?"

Mom looks hurt. She pulls me up and holds it in front of me, fussing with the fabric and smiling wistfully. "Wear it, of course."

"Yeah, it's perfect for playdates and prostitution. Should I move to Nevada? Sign up at a whorehouse?"

"If that's what it takes to get you interested in men again," she snaps. She stops suddenly, and looks into my face. Her eyes widen and her brow furrows in fear. "Oh, unless you've changed teams. But you would have told me if you turned into a lesbian, wouldn't you? Genny?" I push the dress away and exit the room.

As I leave, I hear Daddy scolding her. "The girl lost her husband—in a traumatic way—only two years ago. I reckon she's old enough to know when she's ready to find herself a new one. Leave her be."

SECOND CHANCES

I stay in the hall with my back pressed to the wall, trying to regain a few ounces of patience so I don't punch my mother. God, what was she thinking? Even if I wanted to wear a dress like that again, I can't, not with this body. All that present did was remind me of everything I've lost. Taking a breath, I steady myself and go back into the room.

My father is sitting in his recliner, his eyes glued to the television screen, watching the Cowboys play. CJ is on his lap. "Thanks, Daddy," I tell him, dropping a kiss on top of his balding head.

The man has been balding since I was in high school and he still has just enough hair to do an awful comb over. It's completely obvious, but he's oblivious and I'd never say anything to hurt him. Once, I tried to convince him to just shave his head, but he glared at me and harrumphed, saying nothing else.

My mom takes the baby from my dad, carrying him out of the room and complaining about how mean his Pops and mommy are to her. I sit on the couch and watch football with my dad, still not understanding how the whole thing works.

Shameful, I know, since I live in Texas, but there it is. Cade got so frustrated, trying to explain it to me. Loosing interest quickly, I'd dutifully feign paying attention until I was close enough to distract him with my body—which was way more fun than a lecture on football. Smiling at the memory, I stare at the TV and enjoy the silence. My father doesn't criticize, and he doesn't talk half as much as my mother does.

After ten minutes my mom and CJ still haven't returned and there's a commercial on. My dad clears his throat and asks, "That lawn boy of yours, is he taking good care of everything?"

Lawn boy? I love how even after all the years Daniel's been taking care of the lawn, and doing repairs around the house, Dad still refers to him as the "lawn boy". It's even funnier now that I know Daniel's anything but a boy. He is definitely all man, defending me the way he did at the bar and taking care of CJ when I fell apart. A boy wouldn't do things like that. No, Daniel's turned into a very kind man. I think about the look on his face when he made CJ laugh, but then my mind instantly darts to

SECOND CHANCES

the way his hands felt on my body when we were dancing. I want to banish the thought, but it howls like a banshee.

I hope my voice sounds normal. "He is, Dad. Actually, he fixed that loose board you found the last time you guys were over. Dan's a huge help." I smile when I think about him, the kind of smile I used to have when I was a teenager thinking about a cute boy I saw at the mall.

Dad nods, happy with my answer. "Good. You let me know if he stops working out, ya hear?"

Oh, trust me Dad, I won't be complaining to you about his lack of working out, I promise. Jesus, he's barely legal, I shouldn't be thinking about him—not like this. Where'd it come from? He was a kid—he is a kid. He's in college and I'm in Mommy & Me. We've got nothing in common, except a few moments of something that make no sense. There's no way he has a crush on me. It's impossible. He's just a really sweet guy.

I'm saved from any further lascivious thoughts when my mother comes back into the den, hugging my son close, blowing bubbles on his belly and making him giggle. Seeing him happy makes me smile and I reach up to take him from her, settling him on my lap. He's immediately entranced by the television, watching the guys in tight spandex pants running up and down the field. He doesn't stay with me long, fighting to get down after just a few minutes and toddling over to my dad.

He puts his hands up, saying, "Up! Pops! Up!" He's only fifteen months old, and some words come out clear, like mama. Pops is another. Grandmother isn't exactly flowing from his little mouth yet. I've been telling CJ to call her Nanners. That's what he calls bananas and everyone knows my mom—bless her heart—is a little crazy. He's calling her Nan, which just confuses mom. She thinks he means Nanny, which isn't what she wanted to be dubbed. It's Grandmother or bust.

*****

We spend the rest of the afternoon with my parents, watching football and then eating my mom's homemade meatloaf. The

SECOND CHANCES

woman irritates me to no end, but no matter how upset I might get with her, I'm definitely going over to her house for food. I can make the basic stuff, but she can handle pretty much anything. In my defense, though, when Cade and I were married, he was gone a lot of the time on deployments, or for training, and when he was home, he was perfectly content with steaks cooked on the grill and mashed potatoes. Now that it's just me and CJ, it's easier to make a frozen dinner or scramble some eggs.

After dinner, I help my mom clean up, leaving my father to watch CJ. It doesn't take long for her to start in on me. "So, have you met anyone new lately?" Her tone is hopeful, and I hate that I'm going to disappoint her... again. Since that day I was visited by the chaplain, it feels like nothing I do is right as far as she's concerned. She's always quick to criticize, never noticing how much it hurts. Her support quickly turned to advice, which grew into ridicule as the months passed.

"No, mom, not really." It's not a lie, exactly. I know she's asking if I've met anyone I would be interested in dating, and I might have, maybe. I don't know. It's too confusing. I don't want to think about him, but I do. Daniel keeps popping up in my mind—that smile, those eyes, and that easy way about him. He's just not someone really *new*. Or someone within reach. He's so far out of my league that I might as well try to catch a star with my hands.

She shakes her head, her unhappiness almost palpable. "I know you and Daddy don't think it's been long enough, but it's been more than two years." I lock my jaw, ready to bite her head off. Two years is too soon to put this kind of pressure on me.

"I know that, Mom!" I cut her off, knowing exactly where this conversation is going and really not wanting to hear it. "Do we really need to talk about this again?"

My mother drops the spatula she was scrubbing back into the sink, splattering both of us with soap bubbles, before turning to me with fire brimming in her eyes. "Yes, Genevieve, we do. And we will continue to talk about this until you can explain why you are so determined to be alone. I don't understand you, girl. I really don't."

"I'm not determined to be alone!" I throw my hands up in the air, completely frustrated with the entire conversation. *Just walk away*, I tell myself. But I can't. She doesn't understand and I want her to know. Turning back to my mother, she's disregarded the dishes to study me. Pressing my fingers to my chest, I tell her with my whole heart, "I loved my husband, Mom. He was my life, and he's all I've ever known. What would you do if something happened to Dad? Would you be able to just move on? Find someone new? You wouldn't, so don't ask me to do something when you couldn't do it yourself."

Her eyes soften slightly, but she's still angry with me. "That's not the same thing. Your father and I have been married for over forty years."

"And Cade and I were married for more than ten! I know you've been together longer, but that doesn't mean that you love Daddy more than I loved Cade. That's not fair!" I'm yelling, but, God, she makes me so mad! How can she say it's not the same?

It is, down to the very core. When there's a hole in your heart, you don't want to plug it up right away. I want to miss Cade and I'm afraid of what's next. There's a time to think about what was and what could have been. Moving on skips that part, and means I'll never come to terms with it. As it is, I have nightmares where I wake up screaming, but those aren't the worst of them. The most horrid are the dreams where Cade is alive and talking to me. When I wake, I can't recall what he said, but in the dream I know he's gone, even though he's still right there. It kills me, but I ache for those dreams, for added seconds with him, even if they aren't real.

My father walks in, holding my son in his arms and looking between us. "What is going on? We can hear you shouting in the living room and you're scaring CJ." His eyes are scolding both of us, and I deflate. "Genny, you shouldn't speak to your mother that way."

"I know," I mutter. "But, Dad, she's determined to marry me off again and I'm just not ready." Yes, I am a thirty-three-year-old woman who is tattling on her mother to her father. This is a new low point in my life.

Dad shoos me out of the kitchen so that he can talk to my mom alone. I gladly escape back into the living room and cuddle CJ close to me. "Your grandma just doesn't understand that your daddy isn't replaceable. He's a hard act to follow, isn't he?" I know CJ can't answer me, but just saying it to him makes me feel better about things.

My parents come back into the room a few minutes later, and even though she doesn't apologize to me, she looks like she's been chastised plenty. Sitting beside me on the couch, she takes CJ from my arms, talking gibberish to him and tickling him. She's a completely different person when she's holding her grandson. I just don't get how she can be so mean and calloused toward me, yet so loving to him. She spends most of her time telling me what a failure I am at life, but treats my son like he's hung the moon.

When CJ starts rubbing his eyes and acting cranky, I know it's time to head home. I carry him over to each of my parents so they can hug him and tell him goodbye. I plant a kiss on each of their cheeks, telling them I love them. Since my husband's death, I've made it a point to let everyone know how much I care about them. I want to make sure the people who are most important to me know how special they are. Cade knew how much I loved him, how much he meant to me. I want to make sure everyone else does, too.

Pulling into my driveway, I notice the porch light is glowing even though I forgot to turn it on, and it looks like there's something taped to the front door. Cautiously getting CJ out of his carseat, careful not to wake him, I walk up the path to the front steps. When I get to the porch, I recognize Daniel's handwriting on the note.

Genevieve,

You weren't here when I finished fixing the faucet, so I made sure to turn the porch light on. I also left one of the lights on in the living room since I'm sure you'll be carrying CJ. I didn't want you to freak, thinking someone had broken in. Have a good night, and I'll see you on Tuesday.

SECOND CHANCES

- Daniel

My heart squeezes at his thoughtfulness, not only for turning the lights on for me, but for leaving the note so I wouldn't be scared to go inside. How long has he been making these thoughtful gestures, without me ever taking notice? Not many people would have thought about me and CJ stumbling through a dark room; fewer still would have left a note telling me about it. I take the note from the door and stuff it in my pocket.

Locking the door behind me, I maneuver my way through the toys we left on the floor and I take CJ up to his room. He doesn't even stir when I change his diaper and take his shoes and socks off. I can't get over how much he looks like his daddy, and he looks so peaceful as he sleeps. Leaning over, I press a kiss to his soft skin, making sure to turn the baby monitor on before I leave the room.

I empty my pockets onto the nightstand, strip off my clothes and climb into my lonely bed. Sleep doesn't come easy. I toss and turn for half the night, thinking about Daniel and my late husband, feeling guilty for being happy around Daniel, but being grateful for him at the same time. Enjoying time with Daniel feels like a slap in the face to Cade, even though I know he's gone and never coming back.

Absently, I move to spin my wedding rings on my finger and panic when I realize my finger is bare. There's a white line from the bands sitting on my skin for so long. I didn't wear them today, and it wasn't on purpose. Daniel showed up to fix the faucet and he watched CJ while I showered. After I was dressed, I hurried out of the room, the rings forgotten. I glance at the nightstand and spot them, sitting next to the contents of my pocket, next to Daniel's note.

It kills me when I realize what happened. I curl into a ball and sob into my pillows. "I didn't forget you, Cade, I swear. I won't ever forget you." I clutch the pillow tight and hold onto it like a lifeline. I'm drifting, and feel so lost. How did I forget our rings? I swore I'd always wear them because in my heart I'll always be married.

SECOND CHANCES

The rational part of my brain has been locked in a closet for the past few years, but I hear her through the mental door, *there were days you forgot to wear them when he was alive.*

Finally, sleep claims me. Cade appears in his uniform and walks slowly toward me with a smile on his face. My heart beats hard at the sight of him. In my dream, we are young—the age we were when we got married. He's overjoyed to see me, picks me up and spins me around. I laugh and he sets me down.

Tipping his forehead against mine, he reaches for my hands and when he lifts them, he stops. Pain flashes across his face at my bare fingers, but he swallows it back. Breathing deeply, he says, "It's normal, you know that right? You're not mine anymore, Genevieve. I won't see you again, not for a long time. I love you, baby."

His words ring clearly, even though in past dreams I have no idea what he's said. Then he steps away from me, but I just stand there. He takes another step back, and then another. I scream for him to stop, and hold out my hands, but he doesn't return. I can't move my feet, I can't run to him and make him stay. Cade moves away until he's just a speck and then the blackness swallows him whole.

I wake up in a cold sweat, full of guilt with fresh tears dripping into my hair, and dart upright in the bed, shaking. The blankets can't remove this chill because it feels like my soul is frozen. I won't see Cade again. He's not coming to my dreams anymore and, wherever he's gone, he's finally at peace. He was telling me to do the same, but I can't. Pulling my knees up, I rest my head on them, and wrap my arms around my ankles. Sobs shake my body because I can't accept this. I just can't.

Biting my lip, I look over at my cell. I don't think, I'm too broken to have any thoughts. As if possessed, I pick up the phone and text Daniel.

Sometimes it seems like tomorrow will never come.

Immediately, I regret it. It's the middle of the night—no matter how thoughtful he is, he doesn't want to hear from me at two in the morning. I toss the phone across the bed, not expecting to receive a reply.

SECOND CHANCES

Seconds later, though, the screen lights up. Hesitantly, I crawl across the bed and pick up the phone.

Just breathe, Genevieve. Sometimes you have to live life breath by breath and that's ok. A single tear rolls down my cheek.

I type back *I want to sleep, but I can't. I can't shut out the grief for long enough to shut off my brain. I'm sorry to bother you so late. I don't know why I did it.*

I feel bad for doing this to him. This is my grief and my loss. No one can get to the other side for me. I have to do it myself. The screen glows again.

You're not a bother. I'm here 4 u. Seriously. Now, close your eyes and think of cookies, really big ones. His response makes me smile.

Cookie cars? I reply.

Cookie trains.

Cookie chairs. ☺ *I'd never have any place to sit. I'd totally eat them all.*

And that's why my house isn't made of cookies.

I smile at the phone. *Thank you. Goodnight, Daniel.*

Chapter 9

"Hey, Baby Boy," I coo at CJ, smiling when he grins widely, showing off a few pearly baby teeth. About a week has passed since his fever last broke, and I'm so thankful he's better now. I don't ever want to feel so helpless again. Reaching down, I tickle his tummy lightly, loving his belly laugh. That sound warms my heart. We're sitting on the back porch. CJ is sitting outside on a blanket and playing with trucks, while Daniel pushes the lawnmower across the grass.

Over the past few weeks, I've become keenly aware of the man Daniel has become—and it's not just because he's

SECOND CHANCES

pushing a lawnmower around in my backyard, shirtless and glistening sweat, though that does help. The luster defines his muscles, like he was perfectly cast by the gods and shellacked to endure the ages. I'm sure it's not the first time I've seen him shirtless over the years, but, for the first time, I'm paying attention.

His shoulders are broad, with smooth tanned skin. There's a scar on his upper right arm, a thin white gash that's barely noticeable due to the tattoo that bands around his bicep in an old Celtic pattern. I wonder if he did it to hide the scar or for another reason. It's high enough on his arm that his t-shirt usually covers it. His muscles bulge as he pushes the mower up an incline. My bottom lip is in my mouth and although I'm watching CJ out of the corner of my eye, I can't rip my gaze from Daniel. His jeans hang low on his hips, revealing a black Calvin Klein waistband. The heat and work make the denim damp and heavy. I'd asked him once why he wears jeans all the time when it's a hundred degrees outside, but he just smiled and said something about getting shrapnel tossed at him from the mowers. I think there must be another scar on one of those legs, one that he doesn't want people to see—one that he doesn't want to discuss – and I can't blame him. At least my scars are hidden when I'm not hysterically crying.

I glance down at my hand. I decided to move my wedding band, and only the band, to my right hand. The engagement ring is upstairs in my room. Cade may be gone, but it still means something to me, and that little piece of metal is filled with memories that I don't want to forget. At the same time, things have changed. This little change is a tiny step forward, but it feels like a giant leap. We'd talked about getting an anniversary band, but that wasn't supposed to be for another ten years. This ring wasn't supposed to be on this hand now. I smile at a memory that pops up. It's one of the first times that the sharp blast of colors and shadows isn't accompanied by tears and remorse. Cade was a good man.

I glance up and can't help but notice another good man standing right in front of me. When he's around, I don't feel the age difference between us, even though any

SECOND CHANCES

onlooker could spot it in an instant. I don't want to think about it. Right now, it looks like I'm outside with my baby while the guy takes care of the lawn. No one knows that he's been taking care of me, that we've been texting, and then calling. Daniel has become a bright spot in my day and right now I can't pull my gaze away from the sight of him and that washboard stomach I felt against me when we were dancing. And he's out here broadcasting that beautiful body to anyone who comes by. He knows he looks good, and he definitely knows how to use what he's got.

It's as if Daniel can feel the weight of my eyes on him, because he turns to look at me as he grabs the rag that's been pushed through a belt loop on his pants and proceeds to wipe the sweat off his brow. An image flashes through my mind, uncalled, but it bursts like a firework behind my eyes in a display of glory—I can see myself drawing the pad of my finger over those toned muscles, tracing the rises and falls of his chest down to his waist. I gasp and look away. Where did that come from? My face heats at the thought, I feel like the world's biggest creeper. When I have enough guts to glance up again, I expect him to scowl at me, but he must like whatever he sees on my face, because he smiles and flashes his bright teeth at me.

Why did I check him out? That's what I just did, right? He's too young! I want to smack myself in the head, but it'd be more obvious that I'm crazy, so I just sit there and smirk back. I'm such a creeper. And now that I've noticed him, I can't undo it. I finally see him—all of him—and the splendid way his strong body gleams in the sun. Damn, it's hot out here.

I seriously need to use Lanie's present that's been sitting unopened in the box until now. She bought me a vibrator as a *happy six weeks postpartum* present. Really, who does things like that? The girl is absolutely mental. But thoughts of Lanie vanish when Daniel looks up.

Our eyes lock, causing my stomach to dip as I watch his blue eyes darken from across the yard. It makes my heartbeat quicken and I want to squirm in my seat and press my thighs together, but I don't dare move. He can't know what I'm thinking. What the hell is wrong with me? I look away, but it doesn't help. No man has made me feel this way since Cade. It's been more than two years since I even thought about sex, let alone entertained thoughts of having it. Having your husband die suddenly, leaving you to raise a child by yourself, doesn't do great things for your libido. Not to mention, even thinking about doing *that* with someone other than Cade not only terrifies me, it makes me feel guilty.

Cade should be here. Cade should be the one I'm having these thoughts about. My husband, who is the complete opposite of Daniel, with his blonde hair and brown eyes. He was tall and slim whereas, Daniel isn't quite as tall, but is far more muscular. Cade was strong, there's no denying that, but he was strong in a lanky sort of way, where Daniel's muscles ripple appealingly as he moves.

Oh. My. So my libido isn't dead after all. Things tingle and I feel way too hot as a stupid smile spreads across my mouth. I try to stop it, but I can't, not when Dan's around. Then, it dawns on me that all the calls, the texts—the way we've been flirting. Oh god, this whole time, I've liked Daniel and didn't even notice. My brain didn't think ahead, but that half naked body parading in front of me has pushed my thoughts to the next step. I'm attracted to the man. My lip quivers and drops slightly. How? When?

The realization shocks me to the core. I glance up at him again, and duck my head before he can notice. This feels like middle school. My pulse is pounding and my heart is slapping around in my chest like a wonky tire about to fly off the axle and go flying down the highway. How did I miss it? The way he makes me feel doesn't put us in the friend zone, it's more than that. I feel like a woman when he looks at me, and it makes me feel good. I like it when those blue eyes land on me and Daniel flashes that sexy grin my way. I try so hard to draw it out, and it takes so little for him to offer one.

Cade always said my eyes were the most expressive part of my body, and the last thing I need is for Daniel to know that I'm attracted to him. I'm sitting frozen, with worry pinching my face. This is wrong. My

SECOND CHANCES

friends and family could not accept a relationship like this. I grab hold of my mental reins and yank them back, hard.

My inner voice, the one in the closet, sticks her lips under the crack in the door and says, *It doesn't matter. He doesn't think of you that way, so it doesn't matter. Stop freaking out.*

Now I remember why I don't listen to that part of me. She's annoyingly right, and brutally honest. In this case, she's totally right, and I calm down. I glance up at the sun, feeling the warm light on my face and smile as I let out a long breath of air.

Then everything goes to hell.

The lawnmower stops and the silence nearly knocks me out of my chair. Remember that crazy chick in middle school—the one that had a mad crush on a guy and hid in her locker when ever he walked by?—yeah, that was me. If I hadn't just figured out that I was returning Dan's friendship with a mad crush, I would have invited him in for a drink, but now I'm freakishly frantic to get the baby inside before he can make his way over.

Just as I reach for the door handle, I feel his heat at my back. I stiffen and freeze, feeling an icy chill drip down my spine. A flurry of thoughts flutter through my mind:

Touch me.

Don't touch me.

I'm Cade's.

I want to be yours.

You're too young.

I'm too old.

He's right there, you ass, stop acting like a child and say something!

"Genevieve?" his voice is full of questions I don't want to answer, so I force myself to stand still, facing the door. I can just barely see his reflection in the pane, the concerned frown on his face is obvious. Squeezing my eyes shut, I pray that he will take the silent hint and go away. I'm not that lucky though and there's no way I'm telling him a thing. I'll deny my feelings forever. I can't lose his friendship, it's too important to me. Why did I have to sit out here? If I didn't realize the way I feel about him, this wouldn't be all awkward and weird. I hoist CJ up higher on my hip and try to decide what to do.

SECOND CHANCES

Before I can make a decision, Daniel's hand brushes my arm. Then he takes my hand in his, forcing me around to face him. I'm eye level with his chest and the sight of all that tanned, glistening skin gets to me. Add in the hint of his cologne, mixed with the scent of freshly cut grass and something that's all him. It's intoxicating. I want to lean in and sniff him from his navel to his nose. The thought nearly makes me giggle, but I swallow it back. The result is a stern, gassy look. Wonderful, I look like I'm going to burp.

Dan's hand lingers on mine for just a few seconds, and he offers a boyish smile. It makes me feel like I can fly. Energy that was gone comes surging back and in that instant I think I could run a marathon if it meant I could run into his arms at the finish line. God, I hope he can't tell how much I like him. I take a steady breath and Daniel releases me, but even after he lets go, I can still feel the sensation of his fingers against mine.

Fake it. Fake it. Fake it. Pretend nothing changed. You can do it. Just turn around and say it. I spin on my heel. "Oh, hi Daniel," I say in an attempt to sound nonchalant. I fail miserably, my voice too breathy, like a phone sex operator. But, when I try to lift my chin it's like it's tied to the ground. I'm unable to look him in the eyes. It'll give me away and I'm afraid he'll run if he knows what I'm thinking, how I'm feeling. What twenty-year-old guy wants an old widow with a baby drooling over him?

Daniel bends slightly, tipping his head, and bringing us eye to eye. The look on his face is understanding, like he knows what I'm thinking and it makes me tense a little more. "How's CJ today?" he asks, his concern completely genuine.

We talked last night, so he already knows, but I'm glad he cares enough to ask. I look down at my little man and answer, "He's much better." I try to smile reassuringly at Dan, but it falls flat. All I can think about is how he saw me, and everything in my life, at its worst. Come to think of it, that's all he's seen for a really long time. Some psycho-babbler said the status of your household reflects the inner status of your being. In explanation, my life has gone to hell and so has my living room.

SECOND CHANCES

Dan's seen it all. I've called him in tears and covered his shirt in snot. He probably thinks of me like a second mother or something. Meanwhile I can't stop inhaling his scent. I look like a druggie who found the glue aisle.

Tucking a piece of hair behind my ear, I swing CJ around to my other hip. "Thank you for helping me the other night." I smile, but it feels like someone tied my tongue in knots. "I appreciate the texts and the late night calls. Really, I don't know what I would have done without you. Thank you." The words are hard to say. I hate having to rely on anyone but myself, it makes me feel weak, like I've failed somehow. But, Daniel has never made me feel like that. I called him. We talked, and hearing his voice helped.

Daniel shrugs, as his cheeks turn pink. "No worries. It really wasn't a big deal. I'm glad I could help." He looks nervous now, rubbing a hand along the back of his neck. "Uh...Genevieve?"

"Please, call me Gen," I tell him, feeling much more confident now that he's so obviously unsure.

Clearing his throat, he nods. "Right. So, *Gen*, I was wondering..." The blush on his cheeks gets darker, and I'm really wondering what on earth he's trying to say. A streak of panic races through me. Is there toilet paper hanging from my pants? Do I have something gross on my face? Oh God, did CJ spit up on me and I missed it? But I stand there and smile dumbly, resisting the urge to look at whatever he's trying to tell me is wrong.

Finally, his words rush out and it takes me a moment to decipher what it is he's asking. "Do you want to have dinner with me tonight? You and CJ...not a date or anything, just, uh, hanging out." He continues in a hurry, "We don't have to go anywhere. I could just pick up a pizza and maybe a movie or something?" The way his eyes dart between mine and the ground is adorable, and it sounds like he's asking me on a date at first, until he very clearly clarifies.

At first, I'm too shocked to say anything. I just stand there with CJ on my hip and my jaw dropped.

SECOND CHANCES

My inner voice, Little Miss Logic, is beating the door with a broom, but I'm not letting her out. She yells inside my head, SAY SOMETHING!

Blinking, I snap myself out of it and smile. I look down at CJ to hide whatever expression is on my face. "Oh...I...I don't know what to say. Dinner? As friends?"

"Yeah," he says with a sigh, his shoulders slumping slightly. "I just, I really don't want to go home yet." Something in his voice tells me that his invitation is the equivalent to a late night text from me. Empathy shoots through me and I get it. He just wants some company for a while, and to avoid whatever's bothering him.

That's definitely something I understand. "Okay, sounds great." Turning, I walk inside, before holding the door open and gesturing for him to come with me.

"Do you mind if I borrow your shower before we leave?" he asks sheepishly.

I shake my head. "Of course not. I'm sure you'll feel better after you get all the grass and awesomeness off you."

His dark brow lifts. "Awesomeness?" He tries not to laugh.

"Yeah," I mutter, not knowing exactly where I was going with it. It kind of just popped out. Daniel with no clothes—more awesome than Daniel with clothes. Yeah, I should say that out loud and see how fast he takes off. I laugh it off. "I have mommy brains. I don't know what I'm saying half the time."

He smiles at me for a moment. I can feel his gaze on my back as we walk through the house. I set CJ down in his playpen and pluck a set of towels from the closet and when I get ready to hand them over, Daniel holds up a finger.

"Thanks. One second, I have some extra clothes—let me just go grab them."

Nodding, I watch him jog down the stairs before letting the door shut. Looking down at my son, I see him watching me, his eyes bright. "I guess Daniel's having dinner with us tonight. What do you think about that little guy?" CJ grins, clapping his chubby little hands together so hard that he falls over. I can't help but smile. I rush over and help him sit up again, kissing the top of his head as I do.

SECOND CHANCES

When Daniel comes back inside, he's running his hand through his hair. "I really appreciate this, Gen. I know you have things to do. Are you sure it's okay?" He's standing there, holding a gym bag in one hand, half naked in my foyer.

"Of course it's all right. God knows I've bothered you enough times." No! That came out wrong.

He steps toward me, his eyes locked on mine, his expression serious. "You're never a bother. I've told you that a million times. But this—am I overstepping? I really don't mind if you need space."

"I don't need space, why would you think that?"

He shrugs. "I don't know. The way you reacted before, it was unexpected—like you were disappointed."

Fear sends cold tingles down my spine, but I cling to the smile on my lips like it's a life raft. "Why would you think I was disappointed? Of course not! We love having you here."

"You do?"

"Of course."

He's a step away. I'm not sure how he got so close, but I'm suddenly aware of my loud breathing and I can't remember how to breathe normally. He looks down at me, at my lips, and then lower. My heart slams into my ribs as pins and needles race through my arms. Is he going to kiss me? What the hell is he doing? My stomach flip flops, and when he offers me his boyish grin I melt. "Genevieve?"

"Yeah?" I feel half-drunk with a midlife crisis crush on the lawn boy.

"Can I have the towels, then?"

He's been holding out his hand. Oh God, I misread him. I laugh nervously and shove them into his hands, dropping the washcloth on the floor. "Oh, right! We wouldn't want you walking around naked, would we?" I stoop over to pick up the little cloth at the same time Daniel does and stumble backward, not expecting him there.

He reaches out, grabbing onto me before I fall. His eyes instantly lock on mine as he stops the fall and helps me stand, his slick body pressed to mine. "No, no one would want to see that." He offers a half grin, an expression that I can't read. He holds me a beat too long, but I don't step away either. After a second he swears. "I'm sorry. I've ruined your shirt." He releases me and I look down. My oversized maternity shirt is covered in his sweat, grass, and some grease.

I just smile and tell him, "It's fine. I needed to grab a new shirt anyway. CJ got it all messed up at lunch."

He stands there for a moment. We both do. His gaze makes my stomach flip. If I didn't know better, I'd think he was wondering what's under this shirt, but I know better. He's using me as a hide-out to evade whatever unhappiness waits for him at home. "So, then, I'll just be a second."

"Sure." I watch him disappear up the stairs and let out a huff of air that I didn't realize I was holding. I'm so stupid. I'm acting like a thirteen-year-old. Then it hits me. Flip our ages around and that's what this is like—my feelings for him are like him having feelings for a thirteen-year-old. I lean against the wall and run my hand through my messy hair, while looking down at CJ. "I just want a friend. That's okay, right?"

CJ smiles happily, babbling to himself and then tries to shove a block in his mouth. I watch him, thinking too many thoughts for words. Pushing off the wall, I decide to grab a salad and set the table before Daniel comes out. I'll change my shirt last, because with my luck, I'll spill something all over it. After the table is set and the glasses are filled with ice, I put a few sodas on the table, before heading to the living room. Daniel is changing in my room, so I grab a shirt from the laundry basket, peel off the nasty one, and slip a new, clean shirt over my head. My back is to the staircase and I don't hear anything until the landing creeks.

Whirling around, I see Daniel standing there with a lopsided grin.

Pointing a finger at him, wide-eyed, I scold him. "You did not just watch me change!"

He smiles and slips his hands into his pockets. His hair is still damp from the shower and I swear to God that he's blushing under that gorgeous tan. "I did not just watch you change."

SECOND CHANCES

I smirk and walk toward him. Laughing, I shove his chest. "Liar!"

He laughs with me, holding up his hands. "I swear to God, I didn't see anything. I came down the stairs and when I looked up, you'd already pulled the shirt on. Besides, it's not my fault. I didn't expect to come down here and have you for dinner. I thought we were just friends." He's laughing now, smiling like he can't stop.

"I'm not on the menu."

He kicks the toe of his shoe on the floor. "Well, that's too bad. It would have made an interesting evening." His tone is light and teasing. For the life of me, I can't tell if he's serious or playing.

*****

With both of us cleaned up and feeling human again, we order a pizza and I make a salad so that I'll feel like I had a healthy dinner. Once the food arrives, we sit down at the table to eat. CJ is in his highchair, banging his spoon on the tray while we talk.

"So, why didn't you want to go home?" Maybe I'm prying, but I really want to know.

Daniel puts his slice of pizza down on the plate, looking like this is the last conversation he wants to have. When I start to take back my question though, he shakes his head, holding up a hand to stop me. "It's okay. I don't mind telling you, it's just not a happy story." He runs a hand through his still damp hair before telling me, "My dad isn't thrilled about my choices. He wants me to go work for him, to be a part of his company, and I really don't want to be stuck doing his bidding for the rest of my life. I want to make my own way and be my own boss. I thought he'd understand that, especially since he built his company by himself. But, instead, he's angry. It's a constant battle with him over my landscaping business. He's adamant that I'll never make it. He's waiting for me to crawl back to him and beg forgiveness when I fail. What he doesn't understand is that his constant bitching and yelling just makes me more determined to work harder to prove him wrong."

SECOND CHANCES

I stare at him, my mouth open. I never would have guessed this warm, friendly man is constantly being ridiculed by his father. But, I understand. Poking at a leaf of lettuce, I confess, "I know how it feels to have a parent treat you that way. My dad is awesome, but my mom... she is hypercritical of everything I do. When I got engaged, she told me we'd end up divorced in less than a year. When we moved away to another base, she told me I'd never be able to handle his deployments and it would split us apart. Each time she was wrong, it was like she'd take it as a personal slight and she'd be even more critical the next time."

"But when I lost Cade—I still don't understand why they say *lost*, it's not like I just misplaced him—I had just found out I was pregnant, and she was great. At least, she was at first. Then, she started complaining about what I was eating, how much I was eating, and before long she was back to criticizing everything. If I bought maternity clothes, they were too baggy, or they made me look frumpy."

I laugh, and mimic her voice. "Genny, you need to find a man." Dropping my mom act, I go on, "Like my life won't be good and full unless I have someone to take care of me. It's a complete one-eighty from the way she was while Cade was around. Back then it was all, 'you're too young and you need to live your life before you get tied down.' Now she acts like I'm a spinster that no one wants."

I don't even notice the few tears that started to trail down my cheeks, not until he uses his thumb to wipe them away. He doesn't immediately remove his hand, leaving it cupping my cheek. I can feel my face flush at the way he's looking at me. His eyes are studying me, and I begin to feel naked. Like he can see everything I'm thinking and feeling, like he understands me.

"No one should ever treat you that way," he says fervently, his voice full of conviction. "You deserve so much better than that, Genevieve." The earnest expression on his face is too much and I have to drop my eyes to break the connection.

I still feel his gaze like a caress against my skin, and combined with him touching

SECOND CHANCES

my face, I want to crawl across the table and wrap myself in his arms. He makes me feel so many things that I never thought I'd feel again. The problem is, after two years alone, I have the self-awareness to know that while I want to be as close to him as possible, I'm also terrified of letting someone else in. I don't think I could deal with any kind of loss again. It's easier to stay alone, keeping my distance from everyone and bearing the steady ache in my chest to avoid even the possibility of going through the kind of pain I went through losing Cade.

With the weight of the conversation hanging between us, we come to an unspoken agreement to lighten the mood. Daniel drags me into the living room and pulls me onto the couch beside him. The television flips on and we spend the rest of the night watching some reality show. It's about people who have had deep, loving, online relationships, only to find out that the person they thought they knew wasn't real at all. I'd never seen it before, but by the end of the night, I'm completely hooked. I'm also absolutely positive that online dating is *not* in my future. Sorry, Mom!

Chapter 10

A routine develops where Daniel comes over to work on the yard or fix something in this monster of a house, since something is always breaking, and then stays for dinner. He uses my shower, while I make dinner and then we watch really bad reality television.

Today's no different, except that he brought me tacos from my favorite local Mexican place, and I wasn't expecting him tonight. Luckily, I was only planning on making myself a salad. I'm going to start slimming down this massive mommy butt. Watching sweat trickle down Daniel's back each day has inspired me. Which is good, because it coincides with my mother's force-Genevieve-to-find-a-man plan. She told me all about it when she picked up CJ for the night. She scolded me thoroughly, told me that it was time to lose the thunder-thighs, and walked back down the walk, side by side with my boy, his little fingers wrapped around her pinky.

But, after the emotional assault, I was much more interested in what Daniel brought. Who wants a salad when there's a taco and a burrito with my name on them?

We eat in companionable silence. But, noticing how quiet I am from the fight with my mom, Daniel starts to tease me lightly when we begin cleaning up.

"Here, let me help." Daniel laughs as he makes a move to grab the plates from my hands. Moving faster than I ever thought I could, I manage to keep them out of his grasp, but his arms end up almost around me.

I can't stop the giggle that bubbles up my throat. "No, really. It's okay. I've got it. You did dinner, I'll do the dishes."

"Don't be ridiculous." He's grinning at me with a wonderful smile that makes me want to melt. "I didn't do anything. All I did was pick up the food."

"Really, it's okay. Go sit down and relax! I know how hot it was today, and you spent most of the afternoon outside in the sun." He watches me, but lets me get to the stove thinking that I've won.

Suddenly his hands are on my waist and he picks me up and moves me out of his way, before stepping into my place at the sink and handing me the dish towel. "You dry, I'll wash. Deal?" Still in shock at the way he just manhandled me, I don't respond. I stand with wide eyes, and my jaw dropped, for way too long before a giggly sound comes out of my mouth.

Jabbing a finger at the side of his face, I say, "You did NOT just do that! What the hell, Daniel? All thinking you can come into my house and toss me around like a rag doll." I'm trying to sound angry, but in reality the situation is so unreal that I can't decide if I want to stomp my foot or laugh out loud. The mischievous grin on his face makes the decision for me, and I bust out laughing.

He looks up at me from under his lashes and warmth pools in my stomach. "You are anything but a rag doll." As Daniel says it, he reaches over like he's going to cup my cheek, but instead he drags his cold, wet fingers down my throat, letting drops of cold water drip down my shirt and run between my breasts.

Jumping back, I shriek "Oh my God, that's COLD!" I can't believe he just dripped cold water down my shirt! But, one glance at the smirk on his face tells me that he's not finished yet. He's still standing in front of the sink, a glass full of water in his hand, and I back away slowly. My hands are straight out in front of me, in desperate supplication. "Oh, no. Don't you dare!"

Daniel laughs and steps toward me, and in a rapid move, I'm wrapped in his arms with the cup of water tipped slightly above my head. "Your call, Genevieve. Who's cleaning up dinner? The correct answer is, you are Daniel, the most awesome lawn man I've ever known."

I burst out laughing. "Yeah, I'm not saying that." He tips the cup of water and it begins to dribble down my neck. I gasp and add, "Screw that! I am doing the dishes, not you. So take your tight butt over to the couch and—"

Cutting me off, I can hear the laughter in his voice. "We can discuss my butt later, but you need a lesson in listening and I know just the thing."

"Don't you dare!" He's still holding me tight, my back to his chest. I struggle to get away, just going through the motions. I'm laughing so hard that I'll probably fall on the floor anyway.

"Say it!"

"No!" I laugh and he dribbles more of the water down the front of my shirt. That's when I fight him for the cup and seriously lose. He dumps the rest of the water right over my head.

It drips off the edge of my nose, and my hair is stuck to my face. My shirt is totally soaked and sticking to me like a second skin. I stand there, shoulders hunched, breathing hard. "You're going to regret that."

Darting out of the kitchen, I run to the bathroom, ignoring the makeup running down my cheeks. I lock the door and fill

CJ's bath bucket with cold water from the tub.

Pressing my ear to the door, I listen for any sound that will let me know if Daniel's standing in the hall, but it's dead silent. After waiting a few more minutes, just to be sure, I start to open the door. Before I can even peek through the crack, I'm pushed backwards by Daniel, and bump against the sink. This close to me, I realize just how tall he really is. I have to tip my head back to look him in the eye, and when I do he grabs the bucket from me and holds it above my head.

Just before he tips it over, there's a loud CRASH from the other room. We both stare at each other, eyes wide, for just a second before racing toward the sound. I know it's not CJ because he's with mom, but I can't think of anything that could have made such a huge crash.

We practically skid into the dining room and my hands fly up to cover my mouth. The beautiful antique chandelier is lying, shattered, on top of the dining room table. The floor is covered in shattered glass and crystal.

SECOND CHANCES

"Be careful!" My voice breaks with the emotions I can barely keep inside. There isn't anywhere in this house that doesn't have a memory of my husband. This chandelier was what drew us to the house, and now it's gone, just like he is.

Daniel picks his way around all the broken crystal while I run to get a broom and dustpan to sweep it all up. It physically hurts each time I have to empty the dustpan into the trashcan. It's silly, but it feels like I'm getting rid of another memory of Cade. I start to cry, and god, I'm so tired of crying. I'm transforming into a weepy mess, the opposite of the girl I want Daniel to see.

"Oh, baby, I'm so sorry," he says, coming over to hold me in his strong embrace. Clutching his shirt, I let the tears fall freely even though I know I'll regret it when I'm alone later. I don't even register the endearment he used. Daniel rubs my back, murmuring things I can't make out in an attempt to comfort me. When I finally stop crying, I'm mortified that his light grey shirt is soaked through with my tears. I have got to stop turning into an emotional basket case, especially when he's around.

"I'm so sorry," I whisper, dropping my head in my hands and wishing I could take back the last five minutes. Of course, I got to be in his arms, so I don't really *want* to take them back. It's a vicious cycle of want versus guilt and it sucks. I want Dan, but I miss Cade. I don't know how to sort out the two feelings. Wanting Daniel makes the guilt practically choke me.

Daniel puts his hand under my chin, tipping my head back so that I'm forced to meet his eyes. "Stop that. You don't have anything to be sorry for." He looks uncertain suddenly, but I understand why at his next words. "Do you want to talk about it though? I promise I'm a pretty great listener." His smile is one of my favorite things, and I never can say no to it.

"It's silly, really." He raises an eyebrow, and I know he's saying to tell him anyway, even though he doesn't speak a word. "Okay, fine," I huff when he doesn't give me the out I was hoping for. Or maybe I wasn't hoping for it. Fuck my life. I have no

SECOND CHANCES

idea. "Don't say I didn't warn you." Daniel just smiles warmly, waiting.

"It's just that when we first saw this house, that chandelier was the thing that really sold it to us. I thought it was beautiful, and Cade wanted me to have whatever I wanted. Even when we made plans to do renovations and redecorate the house, we left the chandelier alone. We didn't make it to this room before his last deployment, only getting to the kitchen, the living room, and our bedroom. I haven't been able to bring myself to make any changes to this room because I have so many memories of him here."

A wistful smile spreads across my face as I remember. "The first night we were actually the owners, Cade set up a picnic in here. He had the gingham blanket, the picnic basket, champagne, and so many different finger foods. It was the most romantic thing anyone had ever done for me. It's just hard, you know? I know it's only a light fixture—a thing—but it was attached to so many good times and now it's gone, too. I feel like the objects he touched will all be gone and every memory

I have will vanish." I offer a weak smile and sigh.

Daniel's face is full of compassion when he pulls me into him again. "I can't even begin to imagine what you're going through, Genevieve. You're the strongest person I know." I snort into his shirt because I know he's just trying to make me feel better. Grasping me by my shoulders, he pulls me away from him and frowns down at me. "What was that about?"

"You and your silly questions. Dan, I'm not strong, and you don't need to pretend that I am." I shrug, trying to keep my voice light when really I want to snap at him. "I'm a lot of things, but strong? That's not one of them."

His eyes widen when he realizes I'm serious. "Genevieve, you've been through so much in the past few years: your husband deployed; you found out you were pregnant after having tried for so long; your husband died; you went through your pregnancy alone and raise your son by yourself every day. You've survived all of that, plus your mother." That makes me smile. Dan's gaze is burning with his intensity. "You're so much stronger than you realize. I wish you could see yourself the way I see you. You're fucking amazing. I'm proud to be able to say I know you, and I know Cade was proud to call you his wife."

"You really are the sweetest guy ever," I tell him, unable to tear my eyes away from his. His hand trails up my throat to cup my cheek, and I think he's going to kiss me. Am I ready for him to kiss me? I don't know if I'm up to taking that step, with him or anyone else. But the thought of his lips on mine makes butterflies swirl in my stomach.

He must see the hesitation on my face, because I was certain he was going to put his lips on mine. Instead, he presses them to my forehead in a kiss that is much more like the kiss a friend would give me. I'm shocked by just how disappointed I am that he didn't actually kiss me. He's just a friend. I've been over this in my head a million times. I'm the one misreading his kindness as something more. He doesn't like me that way, why would he?

After the water fight, the broken light fixture—I'm refusing to refer to it as a chandelier in order to keep my sanity—the crying, and the heavy conversation, I'm emotionally and physically exhausted. Daniel notices and says his goodbye, standing on the porch until I lock the door behind him. I shut off the lights on my way up to bed, fall face first into my bed, and am instantly asleep, dreaming of kisses that didn't happen and light fixtures shattering around me.

Chapter 11

"I just want to lick his abs," Lanie groans as she watches Daniel from the kitchen. He's up on a ladder, replacing the chandelier in the dining room.

I'm quickly lost in memories of the afternoon it fell, but Lanie's hand smacking my arm brings me back to the present. She's almost jumping up and down in excitement. "Look! Ahh! Gen! Those abs!" She's so dramatic. When he stretches to hang up the new chandelier, one that looks shockingly similar to the one that broke, his shirt rides up so you can see a portion of what I know is a six-pack. Lanie puts the back of her hand against her forehead, leans her head back and says, "Lord, I feel faint!"

I roll my eyes, but can't help the laughter. You would think she'd never seen a guy's shirt ride up when he lifts his arms with the way she's acting. "Jeez, Lanie, act your age." I sound exasperated, but really I'm just glad that the fight we had is over. I've missed my friend, so when she called to ask if she could come see us, I jumped at the chance to make up with her. Unfortunately, I didn't know she was going to bring my mom.

Mom steps into the kitchen holding CJ's baby monitor. "He's asleep, honey. I brought the monitor in here so you can listen for him."

"Thanks, mom," I say with a sigh. She always acts like I don't know what I'm doing. She's probably right, but I've been his mom for over a year now. We're learning this whole thing together, and she suffocates me sometimes with her *I know everything so you should listen to me* attitude.

She comes to stand between me and Lanie, curious to see what we're staring at. When she sees Daniel in all his glory, standing on the ladder and stretching up to reach the ceiling so that he can screw everything back in, she huffs, shaking her head at both of us. "Girls, y'all are acting like teenagers instead of thirty-year-old women! You should be ashamed of yourselves. The man is only screwing a light."

Lanie laughs until she snorts, elbowing me in the stomach and saying, "I wish he'd teach me how to screw." Oh. My. God. She did *not* just say that in front of my mother!

"Lanie Jo Conrad! Your mama would be shocked hearing you talk like that about a man." My mother constantly feels scandalized by the things that come out of my best friend's mouth. Right about now she's probably wishing we'd never met. "You need to find yourself a nice man and settle down." She narrows her eyes at both of us, "And you better not be giving Gen any ideas."

My face burns, I feel like she just caught me doing something I shouldn't and I hate it. Lanie doesn't let it bother her though; she just hip bumps my mom and says, "Oh come on Mrs. H.! I know you can appreciate the beauty that is a hot, young guy doing the handyman thing. Just look at those muscles! Plus, everyone needs to know how to screw properly!"

"Lanie Conrad! Your mother should wash your mouth out with soap!" My mom is trembling with indignation, her face is red and she looks like she just caught us ogling an underage boy.

Taking her by the arm, I lead her out of the kitchen, exchanging a look with Lanie that says, "This woman is crazy," as we walk past her. As we walk past the dining room, Daniel turns, his eyes meeting mine, lighting up when he sees me.

"Hey, Genevieve." His smile is warm and the sight of that smile causes my stomach to flutter in a way that's not entirely unwelcome. I'm getting used to feeling this way when he looks at me, even though I should be running far away from it.

"Hi, Daniel. How's it going?" I'm trying to keep my cool, but it's not easy. He's wearing jeans that hang loose on his hips and another tight t-shirt, showing off the muscles in his arms.

SECOND CHANCES

"Pretty good. I'll be out of your hair soon." He smiles, as his gaze moves over my body slowly, lighting me up inside before he turns to my mom. "Hey, Mrs. Howlett, how are you?"

Mom lifts her chin, looking down her nose at him. "Hello, Mr. Clement. I'm well, thank you. How's your father?" She's very careful not to ask how he is, and he just barely flinches at the mention of his father. I look at him curiously, wondering if they've had another fight, but he avoids my gaze, keeping his on my mother even as his eyes narrow.

"He's fine, busy with his company." His words are clipped, and his hands tense at his sides before he crosses his arms over his chest, causing a chill in the room. I want to stop her, shut her up before she upsets him more, but I also don't want to call attention to our friendship. She'll never understand why I'd want to be friends with him, especially because he's so much younger. Heaven forbid she finds out that I've got more than friendly feelings for him. I'd never hear the end of it.

She sniffs, "I'm sure he is, especially with this little hobby you have going. Isn't it time you stop playing these games and take your place working with him? You know that's all he's wanted, all these years. He's been waiting for you to grow up."

I didn't think it was possible, but the room gets colder and Daniel tenses even more. I can tell he's angry from the fire in his eyes, and I know I need to get my mom out of here, even though I want to hear more about what's going on with him. He's told me a little about his dad and their relationship, how his dad wants him to work with him, but he hasn't opened up very much about it. No wonder, if this is the way he reacts when someone brings the subject up.

Naturally, I want to know more about him, about what makes him the man he is. Now is definitely not the time though, so before he can say something that will cause even more problems, I usher my mom out of the room and give him an apologetic smile. He glares back at me, but it only lasts a second before his eyes soften.

SECOND CHANCES

"Come on, Mom, Daniel's busy. I'm sure he wants to get this chandelier put up so he can go home—he has better things to do than hang out here in my dining room." I'm hoping she takes the hint and shuts her mouth, but of course, I'm not that lucky.

Instead, she lets out a "Humpf!" before telling me, "I'm so glad you had Cade. He knew how important family is." I close my eyes in mortification, but she keeps right on talking. "I just hope you find a guy more like him, instead of relying on someone like that boy." It's funny now that she's all pro-Cade, but when we were actually together, she did nothing but put him down for the choices he made. She's just the type of person that will never be completely happy unless she's making someone else feel bad.

"Of course, Mom. I'll do my best," I say, trying desperately to placate her and get her out of my house. I can feel Dan's eyes burning into my back as I lead her towards the front door and I quicken my steps. I know that if someone was talking to him about other women, I'd turn green with jealousy. If he feels anything for me, this isn't a conversation he's going to take lightly. It takes everything I have not to release a sigh of relief when I open the door and she walks out onto the porch without protesting.

Putting a hand on my cheek, she gives me a concerned look. "Are you sure you're okay, honey? I know this hasn't been easy on you, raising that baby all alone. I wish you'd let us help you!" Just like that, I feel like an ass for wanting her to leave. She's opinionated and has no tact, but she's my mother and she really does love me, even when she doesn't show it very well. Even when I have to repeat, "she's your mom and she wants you to be happy" like a mantra each time we're in each other's company for more than twenty minutes.

Sagging against the door that I've shut behind me, I nod. "Yes, mom, I'm fine. I just wish you wouldn't be so hard on Daniel. He does a lot for me, and Cade hired him years ago... when he was just a kid. Daniel doesn't have to do all the extra stuff he does, and I feel safe knowing there's a man here." I'm praying she doesn't notice that I'm attracted to him, but she's too busy telling me what I should be doing to notice.

"I know he does a lot for you, and your father and I are grateful to him for it, but if you'd just make an effort, you could find someone! Look at you dear; you're wearing yoga pants and a baggy t-shirt! If you aren't going to take care of yourself and make an effort, no man will either. Why don't you let Maggie set you up with one of those men her husband knows? They aren't Air Force men, and you won't have to worry about them deploying." There's an unspoken, "the way Cade did," hanging at the end of her words.

Holy hell. And we're back to her being her normal judgmental self. I'm ready to pull my hair out and I can't hold myself back anymore. "Will you give it a rest? I'm not looking for anyone right now, I don't need to replace Cade, and CJ is fine with me and only me! It's my family, Mom, not yours. If you don't like the way I do things, then stop coming over." I fold my arms over my chest and glare at her.

Mom's jaw drops at my outburst. Until now, I've been whiny and spineless. We both know it. This wasn't. She raises her nose a little, and sniffles like I've offended her. "I didn't mean to pry, or force you to do something that you don't want to do. I just want you to be happy, and if I've gone about it the wrong way, well, then I'm sorry." She swallows hard and turns to walk back to her car.

Damn it. How does she do it? It's like she took a course for mothers and manipulation. She's an evil genius when it comes to this stuff. I call after her, running down the sidewalk. I touch her arm and say, "Okay, Mom. I'll think about it."

"Do you mean it?" She narrows her eyes at me, scrutinizing both the words I'm saying and my face like she thinks I'm lying to her. I'm not, not really. I will think about it...I just won't actually do it.

"I promise. Now, shouldn't you get home to Daddy? I'm sure he's wondering where you are."

Smiling gently, she nods. "Yes, I'm sure he is. I'll come check on you and the baby in a few days." With that, she kisses my cheek and heads to her car with a

SECOND CHANCES

triumphant smile on her face. Meddling woman. She drives me insane.

After watching to make sure she *really* does leave, I head back inside to where Lanie is still watching Daniel work. His movements are jerky and I can tell he's agitated.

"What did your mom say to him?" Lanie whispers as I come to stand beside her again.

Shaking my head I say, "The usual. He's too young, he needs to do the right thing... you know how she is." Lanie's been my best friend since high school, and even though she pisses me off sometimes, she's the only one who knows everything. Well, everything except the attraction I have to Daniel and the fact that he's been hanging out with me and CJ.

"Girl, I love your mom, but that woman needs a new hobby!" Lanie laughs, but she's right. My mom needs something to focus on besides me, my love life, and the guy who mows my grass. I just don't know what.

Chapter 12

The next few weeks pass quickly. Daniel comes over a couple afternoons a week to do stuff in the yard and help me with projects around the house, staying each night for dinner after showering in my bathroom. I blush every time I think about him being naked...and wet...in my shower.

Daniel never makes me feel like I'm an old lady preying on him. I live for the days he comes over, for the comfortable friendship we've developed. Daniel is the one person in my life that doesn't judge me or my choices. He doesn't tell me how I need to get over it or that I need to date, or find someone new. In fact, the more time we spend together, the more convinced I am that he might be attracted to me. We've spent so much time together lately, watching movies and hanging out, or just talking about our lives.

I've learned that Dan, even though he's a senior in college, is working hard at building his own business. He says he doesn't want to rely on his father forever; he wants to make his own way. In many ways, he's wise beyond his years. We've had so many little moments—moments where his hand brushes mine or when he tucks my hair behind my ear with a small smile, instead of reminding me that I still haven't gotten the haircut I've been talking about.

Being around Daniel is easy. Each night when he finishes whatever he's working on, he comes inside and plays with CJ while I make dinner. The baby is absolutely enamored with Daniel, his eyes follow his every movement and as soon as the door opens he toddles over to meet Daniel as he walks in the door.

Sometimes at moments like those, the guilt is almost unbearable. It tugs at my heart each time, because it should be his daddy he's so happy to see. His dad is supposed to be the one coming in the door and playing with him while I finish dinner. But for my son, he'll never get that experience. He'll never see his dad walk into this house, and he'll never really know him. With that melancholy thought, I look over at my little boy who looks so much like the man I loved with all of my heart.

CJ's sitting on the floor in my room playing with his trucks, while I rummage through my closet looking for something that doesn't scream old, frumpy, or fashion-challenged. I'm having no luck and Daniel will be done in less than an hour based on the sound of the weed eater. I'm tempted to call Lanie and ask for her advice, but if I do, either she'll be over here trying to "help" or she'll call and tell my mother that I'm doing the lawn boy. No one wants that to happen.

Finally, I spy a pair of denim capris that are just tight enough to help keep the little bit of a belly that I still have after carrying CJ from being noticeable, without causing a very unflattering muffin top, and a cream colored t-shirt with brightly colored flowers sprouting from the hem. It's still comfy, and says "I'm not a total hag" without saying "I spent half an hour trying to find something that would impress you".

Once I'm dressed, I study myself in the mirror. I know I'm being extremely critical as I take in all the places that I wish I could change. I know lots of moms see their stretch marks as a badge of honor, but that's not me. Maybe it would be different if I knew the people seeing my body had also seen me before I had a baby. Any guy that sees me naked now would probably run screaming at the silvery lines on my belly, breasts and thighs. I'm pretty certain I have some on my butt too, but there's no way I'm turning myself into a contortionist in an attempt to see.

In addition to the stretch marks, I have a little bit of a pudge. My tummy used to be completely flat thanks to all the cheerleading I did in high school. I don't have the gap between my thighs that I used to have either. I officially have a "mom body" and I haven't come to terms with it. I really need to start going to the gym with Lanie and Erin, but then I'd have to find someone to watch CJ. I'm sure my mom would, but I'm afraid that if she knows I'm going to the gym and bettering myself, I'll come to pick up my son and find random men that she wants to set me up with. Just the thought makes me shudder.

I'm still assessing myself and my outfit when his knock on the front door startles me. *Shit!* He's early! Picking up CJ, I rush downstairs to open the door, breathing just a little harder, my chest heaving slightly.

"Hey," I greet him, trying not to pant. I really should start working out again if just running down the stairs has me out of breath. Maybe I should rethink the whole not wanting my mom to help out. Filing that away in the "things I'll think about later, or maybe never" section of my brain, I concentrate on the man standing in front of me.

Dan's gaze dips down to my chest before he slowly meets my eyes. I can feel the heat rush to my cheeks at the knowledge that he just blatantly checked me out. Clearing his throat, he smiles, "Hey, Genevieve." His eyes light up even more when he sees the baby reaching for him.

SECOND CHANCES

"Hey, buddy," he says as he steps closer to take him from me.

He settles CJ in his arms as the baby starts flailing his arms and babbling at him. Daniel responds to everything like CJ is telling him all about his day, saying things like "really?" and "you don't say!" I shoot him a glare when I hear "Your mom did what?" and he chuckles.

When CJ starts saying "Dadadadadada," I have to squeeze my eyes shut to keep the tears at bay. I know he's not really calling Daniel "Daddy", he just can't say "Dan", but it still makes me feel so *guilty*. Logically, I know that he calls my dad "dada" half the time instead of "pops". It doesn't make it any easier though. Luckily, Daniel is engrossed in what my son is saying to him and doesn't notice the look on my face.

Stepping back, I gesture for him to come inside. Daniel walks past me, pausing in his conversation with CJ to brush a light kiss on my cheek in hello. I should be used to these by now. The first time he kissed my cheek was the night he walked in on my embarrassing breakdown.

Since then, he's shown affection in small ways each time he's been here. A kiss on the cheek, the top of my head or my forehead, or even just a light brush of his knuckles down my cheek as he says goodnight. It's not much different with the baby. He frequently places a kiss on the top of CJ's head before he leaves, but it feels different when he does it to me. I have to admit though that I love how Daniel shows affection. I know it's wrong to keep comparing him to my husband, but I can't help it. Cade was affectionate, to a point. He was very straight-laced and perfect for military life. He would cuddle with me when we were alone, but around other people, he'd barely even put his arm around me.

Instead of stopping in the living room, Daniel continues straight to the kitchen where he sits CJ in his highchair, making sure he's safely secured, before helping get the meatloaf and mashed potatoes on the table. He pulls my chair out, waits for me to sit, and then takes his own seat. Our conversation during dinner is as comfortable as it always is, Daniel tells me about his classes this week, and the houses he's had to visit to either maintain the landscaping or discuss new projects.

He's so creative. He actually brought his portfolio over the last time he was here. We spent the entire night going over each picture, him telling me stories about the clients and how he came up with different designs. His landscapes look like works of art, much more elaborate than what he's done here. When I asked him why, he told me that my husband had told him to make it simple, something I could take care of on my own if needed. I don't think Daniel realized what he'd been thinking, but I did. Cade was making contingency plans in case he was deployed and didn't come home. He was always thinking ahead, planning for the worst even if he never said that.

Daniel makes me laugh when he talks about his classmates and how his roommate smuggled a goose into the dorm. It escaped and chased a couple of girls down the hall, squawking its head off. I always forget that he's so much younger than me, because he doesn't act like a twenty-two-year-old. Daniel is more certain of himself, and there's something else too—the residue from life lingers on his shoulders the same way it does for me. It seems to close the age gap. I don't know what tarnished him to make him seem older, or maybe that's not it at all. Maybe it's from taking care of his sister for so long. He was forced to grow up much faster than he should have.

Dan's face is animated, his arms moving around, as he explains a particularly difficult customer, one who is never happy with what he does, even when it's exactly what she wanted. "If I can ever make that woman happy, I'll die of shock."

"Maybe she just wants an excuse for you to come back," I say with a laugh. I can totally see that being the case. Not to mention, he's a young guy, who even though he's in college, owns his own business and works harder than anyone else I know. I bet every woman in San Antonio is after him. Just the thought makes me grip my fork tighter in jealousy even though he's not mine.

Daniel laughs, but I know I embarrassed him because a faint pink color races across his cheeks as he avoids my

SECOND CHANCES

gaze. I start to apologize, but he waves it off. "Don't worry about it, Gen. You're probably right anyway."

I smile up at him because he's never acknowledged the way women want him before. I don't say anything though, after all, what can I say? I'm one of them. With a shrug, Daniel starts to clear the dishes off the table, leaving me to take CJ up for his bath and to get him ready for bed.

Chapter 13

Once CJ is bathed and in bed, I head back downstairs to find Daniel sprawled out in the middle of the couch, his long legs stretched out in front of him and his arms spread out along the back. Daniel's head snaps up when he hears me, and I feel self-conscious having him watch me walk towards him. Sitting beside him, I curl up on my side of the couch pulling my legs up underneath me, careful not to touch his arm resting on the back of the couch behind me.

Once he's sure I'm comfortable, he hits play and one of my favorite movies, *Casablanca,* starts to play. I look over at him, my eyes wide in surprise, but he only shrugs. "You said the other day that you love this one and haven't watched it in a while. I've never seen it, so I picked it up on my way over tonight."

For a few minutes, I'm speechless. I have no idea what to say. I'm surprised that he remembers a comment I made almost a week ago in passing, and that he volunteered to watch it. We sit, side by side, and soon I'm engrossed in the movie. About thirty minutes in, Daniel turns so that he's almost sideways, giving me an unobstructed view of his handsome face.

"So, what's the draw to this movie?" he asks, studying me seriously.

His question surprises me. I don't think anyone has ever asked why I like this old movie, so I've never had to think about the reasons. I shrug, "I don't know." When he continues to study me, saying nothing, I stop to think about it for a second. "It's romantic, but it's real too. Life doesn't go as planned, but somehow they find love anyway. And it's nostalgic too. I watched these when I was younger and carefree—they remind me of the good times."

He nods and turns back to the screen. Before I can ask, he turns back to me and says in a low voice, "I can't remember a time when I didn't feel like I was responsible for everything." I know I'm staring at him with wide eyes, afraid to ask him why because I don't want him to stop talking. After a few moments of silence, he continues, "I told you before that I have a sister," he pauses, and I nod my head. "She's younger than me by a few years. My parents used to argue all the time. My dad is a real hard-ass. Always telling my mom where she was allowed to go, who she could go with, and how long she could be gone. My mother was the type of person who would do things spontaneously, so she hated being collared like that. We'd be out shopping and she'd decide to stop at a park or an ice cream shop on a whim, never thinking about how he'd react."

The arm that's not resting along the back of my couch tightens into a fist as he remembers something. I reach out to take his palm in mine, trying to relax him. He looks down at our fingers entwined together and smiles softly before taking a deep breath. "One day, she just snapped. She was tired of him treating her like that and she just left. Melody and I came home from school and it was like she'd never been there."

"Oh, Daniel," I start, but he shakes his head.

"Don't feel sorry for me. I understand why she left. I just don't get why she never came back for us. Once it was just the three of us, my father started spending more time at work and leaving me to take care of Melody. Now, he's almost as hard on me as he was on her. The thing is, he got worse after she left. One day I got into his things, his prized collection of cats."

My eyebrow shoots up. "Cats? As in stuffed kitty cats?"

He laughs once, but it's sad. "If only. No, he collects cat o'nine tails and other sailing crap from a million years ago. They usually go straight into a glass case, but one day I went into his office and it was just sitting on his desk. I picked it up to look at it. I knew the thing was a weapon, but I didn't really get how it worked. Dad showed up and decided the best way to teach me not to touch his stuff was to show me how it worked." He hikes up the cuff of his jeans and I can see the start of a scar. When he pulls them a tad higher, I can see more.

My hand flies to my mouth in horror. He whipped his son? With a real whip? Those things rip the skin off. It's worse than being whipped. "Oh my God." My voice trembles as I stare at him slack-jawed.

He yanks his pant leg down. "Now you know why I always wear jeans. It's easier than to answer the endless questions about the scars on my legs." He smiles sadly, staring into space, and then looks back over at me. "Now, he's demanding that I go work for him when I'm out of school, but that's the last thing I want. I don't want him to ever be able to control me again. The only reason I still put up with his shit is so I can make sure Melody is okay."

Daniel's arm has moved so that it's resting along my shoulder, his fingers rubbing small circles along my skin and raising goose bumps.

It takes everything in me not to react to his touch, but I can't quite stop the way my body stiffens at the feel of his fingers. After a few minutes he moves his arm so that it's no longer touching me and I miss the feeling. It's been so long since a man touched me, since I felt this way about being caressed. The thought brings the feeling of ice rushing through my veins as I remember those last few minutes with Cade. Cade, who never would have sat through *Casablanca* with me without protesting loudly. God, he hated these kinds of movies. If it wasn't action, or suspense mixed with romance, he tuned it out.

It feels like I'm being torn in two inside. I want to let go of my past, but there's no way Daniel's my future. I'm not even sure why he comes by day after day. I dress like a slob, and the house is falling apart. No one can tell I have a cent to my name, and yet he comes back again and again.

"Why are you here, Daniel?" my voice is quiet, but in the darkness of my living room, the only light coming from the black and white movie playing on my television, it sounds like a shout.

His head whips around and his eyes meet my questioning gaze. He's wary and a little unsure. The confident smirk that's normally on his face is gone. In its place is a young man who looks convinced he's about to be scolded. "What do you mean?"

"I mean, why are you here when I'm sure there's plenty of other things you'd rather be doing instead of sitting here watching an old movie with me?" I look down quickly; not wanting to see the relief on his face that I'm positive will be there, now that he knows he doesn't have to stay – that I don't expect him to.

I'm completely unprepared for his hand under my chin, lifting my face up to meet his earnest gaze. "Genevieve, there's nowhere else I'd rather be than right here with you." He swallows hard. "Can I tell you a secret?"

I shiver and feel as though a premonition hits me hard, but I nod. "If you like."

Glancing at his hands, he confesses, "I've had a crush on you since I was fifteen. I'm here because it's my favorite place to be." When he looks up, our eyes lock. My

SECOND CHANCES

heart pounds hard and fast. I can't fatnom what he's said.

Unable to do anything but stare wide-eyed at him, I don't pull away when he inches closer and closer—his eyes darting between my lips and my eyes. He's careful and slow, giving me plenty of time to escape, but I don't. Daniel lowers his face closer to mine and brushes his lips softly across the seam of my mouth. He's hesitant and gentle as he moves, acting like he might spook me at any moment. When I lean into him, Daniels's hand comes up to cup my cheek. The rest of the world and all my worries about my past, our age difference, and my late husband fall away under the soft pressure of his kiss.

The tip of Daniel's tongue traces the bow of my lips, the sensation causing me to gasp and grip his biceps tightly. He takes advantage of my open mouth as his tongue darts in to touch mine. As our tongues tangle together, I slide my hands up and around his neck, pulling him closer. I'm expecting him to lay me down on the couch, so when his hands go around my waist, lifting me up and setting me down with a knee on each side of his hips and making me straddle him, I yelp.

He breaks away from me long enough to chuckle before crushing his mouth to mine. It's rougher than the first kiss, more sure this time. It's insistent and passionate, making me feel sexy and beautiful—two things I haven't felt in a very long time. My hands are gripping his shoulders while his hands rest on my thighs, something that would normally make me feel very insecure, but somehow, even though he's running his hands up and down my legs, it makes me want to get closer to him.

When his hands move back to my waist he pulls me down so I'm seated more firmly on his lap and able to feel how much he wants me. He doesn't try to hide it at all. I whimper into his mouth and his hands tighten as they begin rocking me back and forth, guiding me until I get the rhythm. When I'm moving on my own, he starts sliding his hands up my sides until his thumbs rest just under my breasts, making me arch into him, begging for his touch.

Daniel and I are wrapped up in each other, completely disregarding the world around us, until a sharp gasp brings us crashing back down to reality. Whipping my head up, I see my mother standing in the doorway to the living room, a hand covering her mouth in shock. Hurrying to stand, I straighten my shirt which has been pushed up to just under my breasts and pray I don't look as mortified as I feel. "Mom," I gasp as I get to my feet.

Daniel gets up slower and stands behind me, placing his hands on my shoulders in silent support. My mom stares hard at the spot where he's touching me, before finally meeting my eyes. I can see so many emotions tear through her in that moment—worry, anger, horror, and worst of all disappointment.

"What on earth are you doing, Genny?" Her voice is shrill and shocked.

My face flames in embarrassment, but before I can answer, Daniel says, his voice still rough from our make-out session, "Ma'am, with all due respect, we are both adults and what we were doing is our business."

She practically vibrates with anger at his words. Walking closer, she grabs my hand and yanks me away from him so that I'm standing beside her. Then she points a finger at his chest. "You are barely an adult Mr. Clement, and I won't stand by and watch you try to take advantage of my daughter!"

I'm looking back and forth between them; completely confused at the way she's decided to play this. "He is not taking advantage of me!"

"Yes, he is, and he knows damn well what he's doing."

Ready to pull my hair out, I screech, "What are you talking about, Mom?"

Spinning around, she sets her glare on me. "I'm talking about him thinking that he can seduce you right out of the money that Cade left you. That boy—" she gestures back towards Daniel, who's staring angrily back at her "—is trying to spite his father, and thinks he can use you and your husband's insurance money to do it! All he has to do is get in your pants and it's as good as his."

My mouth drops open in shock. "No, he wouldn't…"

SECOND CHANCES

"Genny," Mom interrupts, "you were always naïve, but really, this? You know his reputation. Where do you think it came from?"

I knew he had a reputation as a ladies man, but the guy is walking talking candy. I didn't really think anything about it. What guy wouldn't take advantage of super good looks? Besides, I can't believe he would do that, not until Mom tops her argument with the cherry that haunts me every time we're together.

"Think about it, dear. Why would a young, handsome guy spend so much time with a widow ten years his senior and her child?" Her gaze slips over my body, at the clothes I'm wearing, and I know I look frumpy. She says exactly what I've feared the most, that he could be using me for some reason. Maybe he saw a notice from the insurance company. He's in the house enough that he could have seen a bank statement, that he could have figured it out.

When I don't immediately defend him, Daniel takes a step towards me, his anger almost palpable. His eyes are narrowed, and his hands are both fisted at his sides.

"Genevieve," he begins, and I flinch at his use of my full name. He stops, clearing his throat and squeezing his eyes shut for a second, before addressing me. "Gen, you know me. I would never do that to you, and I would never disrespect Cade that way."

His voice rings with conviction and I want to believe him in the worst way. Sensing my wavering feelings, he reaches out to me, but my mom steps between us. Turning her back to him, my mother faces me, her mouth pinched in disapproval. "Genevieve Prior!" I stop looking around her and meet her steely gaze. "What are you thinking? Cade wouldn't want this. You deserve a man who will take care of you and CJ, not a boy who wants you to take care of him." She shakes her head and her obvious disappointment in me stings. "You are old enough to know better! Think of CJ! That money is for him to have a good life. You can't let the help use you and walk off with it."

"Now, wait just a minute!" Daniel seethes. "You don't know anything about our relationship. I don't care if you are her mom, that doesn't give you the right to talk down to her like that, and you sure as hell aren't talking to me that way. I don't give a damn about how much money she has or doesn't have. Money is a non-issue for me—"

Before he can continue, my mother holds up a hand. "I would prefer it if you left Mr. Clement. Don't presume to know my daughter or her feelings. In fact, I think it would be best if you looked elsewhere for lawn care clients." Putting an arm around my waist, she pulls me close to her so that we are standing united against Daniel. I'm so confused that I say nothing. Every worry I ever had about him races through my mind. I knew there had to be a logical reason he was here, and this is it.

Or he loves you, the back of my mind whispers, but I can't hear it. It's so much easier to believe the worst. I can't take another heartbreak and the words my mother planted in my mind took root.

"Seriously? You're going to believe this crap?" At first he thinks I'm going to blow it off, but when I don't defend him, his spine stiffens before he curls forward ever so slightly—as if he were sucker-punched right in the stomach. The look he gives me makes my heart clench painfully in my chest.

"Dan, how do I know? Just say it. Tell me why you're here."

His jaw locks and he presses his eyes closed like he can't stand the sight of me. Finally, he sucks in a chunk of air and shakes his head, his mouth twisted into a wounded smile. "I poured my heart out to you and this is what I get in return. You know what?" he asks, looking at both my mother and I, "I don't need this shit." He huffs out a dark laugh that's more disbelief than anything else. Turning his angry stare on me, the look in his eyes causes me to shrink back into my mother. "I told you things I've never told anyone else. I thought I could trust you. Guess I was wrong." With one last look, he destroys me. "Have a nice life, Genevieve." Slamming the front door behind him, he's gone.

He left.

"Hmpf." Walking over to the couch, my mother sits on it, patting the seat beside her, letting me know she wants to talk.

SECOND CHANCES

"No. Not now, and I swear to God if you ever do anything like this again—" I feel sick. My stomach tightens and churns. What if she's right and he was after my money? But what if she's wrong? I just let a great guy walk away, and not only that, I let him think I believe he was using me—that he's a thief.

"Like what? Point out the obvious? Come on Genny, you're not a little girl anymore and that guy isn't Cade. Just because he flirts with you and makes funny faces at CJ doesn't mean anything."

I'm losing it. She should leave, but she just sits there. I start screaming. "What if you're wrong? What if he does care? What if he really wants CJ and me? What then, Mom?"

"Then, he'll come back." She seems so certain. If someone I cared about suggested I was a gold-digger, I wouldn't go back. Fuck that. Shit, that's exactly what he said. Oh god, I feel sick.

Mom studies me intently, but finally stands, coming over to kiss my forehead. "I'm sorry, honey. I didn't mean to meddle. I never thought he'd actually make a move on you. You know that's why his father is putting so much pressure on him, right? Because the kid is broke and his dad is bailing him out. Mr. Clement is a good man, but I've heard things about his son. I couldn't ignore it any longer, not after I saw you two together. I am sorry, Gen. I'll come over in the morning and we can figure things out, okay?" Her earlier pique is forgotten now that she's gotten her way. She grabs her purse off the table by the front door and leaves, closing the door quietly behind her. I am alone with my thoughts.

Sinking down onto the couch where just an hour ago I was happier than I've been in a long while, I lift a shaky hand to my lips, still able to feel his kiss. What have I done?

Chapter 14

It's been almost a week since Daniel walked out of my life, but it feels longer. I don't know what to think. Truth be told, I had a hard time believing that he really wanted me. I still do. I mean, look at me—I'm a thirty-three-year-old widow with a baby. I don't have the body of a woman his age, and I have a lot of baggage. My body is far from perfect, and I'm a lot curvier than I was when I was his age. Add in the stretch marks, droopy boobs, and my saddle bags, and it's hard to see what he saw in me. Daniel either weaseled his way into my life at my all-time low or he saved me. Those two things shouldn't be difficult to tell apart, but it's harder than you'd think. My ego would fly knowing he chose me and I'd be crushed if he were here because of my bank statement—which I never thought to keep hidden.

Running a hand over CJ's blonde hair, I smile softly down at him. I love him to pieces and have spent the past few days rolling around on the floor, trying to make him laugh—trying to forget about Daniel. CJ knows I'm sad, because he throws those chubby arms around my neck and makes faces that always get a chuckle out of me before he returns to his toys. We talk about things and sometimes I talk about Daniel.

CJ hands me a block and gestures for me to put it by my ear. He picks up another and does the same. I smile at him. "Hello, is CJ there?"

"Mamamamama."

"Yes, this is Mama. How are you today?"

"Pppppllllbbbbb."

"Yeah, me too. We should hang up and go get some ice cream. What do you say to that?" He throws the block with a whoop, and claps! "Yeah, I thought you'd like that."

SECOND CHANCES

After I get him in his chair, we make sundaes. His is mostly one little scoop of vanilla ice cream and a mound of whipped cream. I hand him a spoon, but he's so excited that he plunges face-first into the mound of sugar. Laughing, I say, "Wait! Wait!"

He looks up at me, his little face covered in cream, with that little lower lip quivering. I was going to tell him to use his spoon, but I smile instead and tell him, "It's good, isn't it?" He's still ready to cry. "Should mama eat it like that too?" I get a vigorous nod.

I put more whipped cream on mine and hesitate. CJ is watching me closely, his little eyes widen and I can see hope dancing across his little face. Ignoring my spoon, I plant my face in the whipped cream and take a bite. He's quiet until I look up, my face covered in foamy white cream. He giggles hysterically and goes back to eating his own sundae. When I stop, he prods me. I laugh and eat my food like a dog, licking and chomping at it, until CJ and I are hysterically laughing and the ice cream is everywhere.

My phone rings. I glance over and see my mom's name pop up. I ignore it. We haven't spoken since the night she caught Daniel and me, and I'm in no hurry to chat with her. My eyes snap back to the phone when it stops and immediately starts ringing again, and I get an awful feeling in my gut. My skin prickles and a shiver takes hold of me. I stare at the phone like it's evil. I don't want to answer. Something's wrong, I can feel it.

"Hello?" The next few words shatter everything I know and my hand starts shaking so badly that I barely register that mom is speaking.

My mom's voice is heavy with remorse as she says, "Genevieve, please answer me. You need to get to the hospital as soon as possible. It's your father. I hate to tell you the news this way, but there's very little time left. Please come down here."

I don't really know what happens over the next thirty minutes. But as I pull up to the hospital, I vaguely recall calling Lanie and asking her to come stay with CJ. My mother didn't tell me exactly what was going on, but her tone was enough to jolt me into action, no matter what's going on between the two of us.

My father has been my rock since Cade's death; he's the one who held me together when I thought I would crumble. Losing him so soon after my husband is unfathomable. Especially now that I've pushed Daniel away too.

He's not dying. You don't know that. Stop thinking the worst. Go find him. Rational me is yelling inside my head. I really need to let her out, but I don't think she can handle what's coming. I feel it.

Hurrying over to the information desk, I ask for Michael Howlett, but before she can even look it up I hear my name. Whirling around, I see my mom, tears streaming down her face and I run to her.

"What is it? You didn't tell me anything when you called. Is he okay?" The questions are flying out of my mouth faster than she can answer them and finally she covers my mouth with her hand and gives me an exasperated look. Granted, it's subdued by the tears streaming down her cheeks, but I'm used to this look and it calms me somewhat.

Taking my hand, she leads me to the group of elevators down the hall. "Oh, Gen, I don't know how to tell you this honey."

My heart clenches at the utter misery in her voice. "What? Please Mom, just tell me!" I'm starting to become frantic now. It reminds me of the way the chaplain slowly told me that Cade was gone. They didn't burst into the room and spit it out. They came to it slowly, so that I knew what happened before he even said it. It was kinder that way, but the memories swirl behind my eyes and fear chokes me. This can't be happening.

"Is he going to be okay?" I ask, my voice trembling. It's the only thing I can think to ask and the only thing that she's not telling me. Maybe he's already gone and she doesn't know how to explain that I'm too late. Mom leads me down the hall. She doesn't respond until we're in the elevator and it begins to move.

"Oh, honey," she shakes her head and I swear I stop breathing. "No, he's not. They said he doesn't have much time left, but I wanted you to be able to say goodbye." My legs wobble, but I'm able to stay upright as my mom clutches both of my hands in hers.

The elevator dings and she leads me down the hallway. It seems to get longer and longer the further we walk. I'm beginning to tremble when she finally reaches the room. Nothing in the world could prepare me for seeing my father lying in that hospital bed, wires sprouting from what looks like everywhere, and a machine beeping with each heartbeat.

It's all I can do not to break down at the sight, but I know I need to stay strong for my mother. She looks like she's ready to fall apart. Together we walk to his bedside, each clutching the other's hand tightly. Tears are streaming down my face as I look down at my dad. His eyes are closed and it's strange to see him lying so still. He's the kind of person who is always moving, always doing something. If I would've let him, he'd have done every project I needed done at the house instead of having Daniel do it, but I wanted to do it on my own. I wanted him to know that he didn't need to worry about me.

"It's his heart," Mom whispers, her voice trembling. My own heart squeezes because I know it's bad. He's had two heart attacks in the past few years, and after the last one they told us his heart most likely wouldn't survive a third.

I suck in a shaky breath, before asking, "How long does he have left?"

She shrugs, before sucking in air and trying to steady herself. "The machines are the only thing keeping him here. They said he won't wake up. I just wanted you to have the chance to say goodbye." A sob escapes her. "Oh, Genny, what am I going to do without him?"

Even though we've been fighting, I let it all go—everything. I can't let her stand here, knowing that she's about to lose her husband of forty years, and not comfort her. Wrapping an arm around her shoulder I pull her into me. She clutches my waist as sobs overtake her and her entire body begins to shake. There's nothing I can do to make this better, to make any of this easier, but at least I can be here for her.

After a few minutes, she lets me go and moves away, wiping the tears from her cheeks. She lifts her chin, and this is the mom I'm familiar with. The hard ass, the one who never lets anything affect her. "I'll give you a few minutes alone with him," she states before walking away from me.

The door clicks shut softly behind her, leaving me in here, alone with my dad. Pulling the solitary chair that sits against the wall over to the bed, I sit, taking his big hand in both of mine. My father has always seemed larger than life, a big bear of a man. But right now, he seems small. Instead of the smile he always had for me, and the booming laugh that he was quick to use, he's still... and silent.

"Hey, Daddy," I start, having to clear my throat before I continue. "I can't believe this is happening right now. Don't you know how much I need you? How much it tears me up that CJ is never going to get to really know you? He just started saying your name." My throat is thick with the sobs I'm trying to keep at bay, but it's a losing battle. Thinking about the fact that my son will never remember my father completely crushes me.

Turning his hand over, I trace his large fingers with mine, committing the feel of his hand to memory. These are the hands that picked me up when I fell down, that held me as I went through the hardest moments of my life. These hands were one of the first to hold my son, and God, he was so proud that day. I swear his chest puffed out as he looked down at his grandson for the first time.

"I'm your Pops!" he told CJ, his big voice startling him. That's one of my favorite memories of Daddy. That one, and the one of him walking me down the aisle on our wedding day. He was so happy. My dad loved Cade. He was the son he never had, the son he could take fishing or hunting, who he could watch NASCAR with.

I don't even notice the tears streaming down my face and falling onto our hands. This is the last time I'll touch my father. How is that possible? And why am I so focused on his damn hands?! I know my mom is going to be back in just a few minutes, so it's time to say goodbye.

SECOND CHANCES

"I love you, Daddy. Say hi to Cade for me, and be sure to tell him all about our little boy, okay? I'll make sure CJ knows all about his Pops and how much you loved him. I love you, Daddy." I choke on the final words and it takes a few tries for me to get them out. "Sleep well." Leaning over, I press a kiss to his warm cheek before standing up to get my mother.

I leave as she enters, giving her a few final moments with him before they turn off the machines. It doesn't take long, but I stand in the room beside my mother, our hands clenched together as we hold each other up. When the beeping slows, I can feel her shaking increase, but the worst is when it stops altogether. Mom's legs give out and we both sink to the hospital floor. The nurse in the room asks if we need anything, but I just shake my head. There's nothing she can do for us now.

We sit there on the floor for what feels like hours, while my mom cries for the loss of her husband and I cry for the loss of my father. Finally, her sobs quiet, and we help each other up.

Straightening her back, my mother walks over to the bed where my father's body lays and she presses a final kiss to his lips. "Goodbye, Michael. I love you," she says, as she trails her knuckles down his cheek before squeezing his hand once. Taking a deep breath, she turns her back on him and comes to me. "Take me to my grandson, Genevieve," she says, her voice stronger, but brittle.

Someone had already spoken to me about the funeral arrangements and who to call. I told them that I'd take care of everything. We're supposed to say our goodbyes and the next time we see him will be at the viewing. I understand why she wants CJ. The hugs of a baby are healing for the soul.

Nodding, I follow her out of the hospital room and back downstairs. We take my car back to the house, and Lanie doesn't even have to ask what happened. It's written all over our faces. Fat tears roll down her cheeks as she embraces me, while my mom heads straight for CJ. Lanie keeps her arms around me as we watch my mother cuddle my son, oblivious to our

SECOND CHANCES

stares. I've never understood how she can seemingly turn off her emotions so easily, but today, I wish I had that ability. I feel like someone shoved a pitchfork through my heart.

Lanie and my mom both stay the night at my house, and I'm so thankful that I'm not alone. I wish Daniel was here to hold me, but I can't call him, I can't. We don't mention what happened today and I know it's because my mother is in denial, but I figure she deserves one night to not think about it. Especially since the next few days she's not going to be able to get away from it, no matter how hard she tries.

By the time I slip into bed at night, I'm exhausted. The kind of exhaustion that I haven't had since the Air Force came to tell me about Cade. I've been through all this before and now I have to get my mother through it as well. I just hope I'm strong enough to hold both of us up.

Chapter 15

I've been dreading this day since Daddy passed away. The past two years have been full of heartache and pain. I'm ready to see the other side of the coin. In two years, I've lost the love of my life and my dad. It just doesn't seem fair. I don't understand why I keep losing the men I love. First Cade, and now my father. I can't fathom it, so I stop trying.

CJ and I have spent the past three days at my mom's so she wouldn't be alone. I feel bad about it, but I'm more than ready to get back to my own house. My mother is a neurotic control freak on a good day, but it's been heightened by about a thousand since my dad passed.

"Genny," she calls from down the stairs, and I groan inwardly at the possible reasons she's calling for me. Since we got here, she's needed me to go through Dad's closet to pick his outfit, take it to the mortuary, contact all the family she could think of, plan the after-funeral meal that will take place here at the house, and so much more.

Sighing, I make my way to the top of the landing so she can see me. "Yes, Mom," I answer, eager to get it over with. Mom is standing at the bottom of the stairs, wringing her hands together, wearing a fitted black dress and a hat box hat complete with black veil. That's my mom... she does mourning right. Meanwhile, I'm dressing, once again, in yoga pants and a t-shirt. At least the t-shirt is clean this time.

"Honey, Mitch is here from the funeral home, to set things up for after the funeral this afternoon. Can you show him where to put all the chairs? I just..." she covers her mouth with a hand as tears start to course down her cheeks. "I just don't think I can handle it." Her eyes are pleading.

"Of course, Mom."

She leads me over to where they're setting things up for later. As I start to move past her, she grips my arm so tightly that I'm pretty sure she's cutting off all circulation. "You know, Genevieve," she says in a syrupy, sweet voice. "Mitch is a nice man and, since he already has kids he probably wouldn't have a problem with you already having CJ." She winks at me as I realize that the whole crying and pleading eyes thing was just an act to get me alone with Mitch.

I don't know how she knows all this information about him and I cringe inwardly at the possibilities. I wouldn't put it past her to send out one of those, "applications to date my daughter" forms that you see online.

Shaking my head in disbelief, I jerk my arm out of her grasp to hiss at her, "Please drop the matchmaking Mother. I can't deal with it on top of everything else." She has the decency to at least look chagrined, but she doesn't apologize for her actions.

SECOND CHANCES

I walk over to where Mitch stands, looking extremely uncomfortable after obviously hearing my mother's comments. I have no idea what to say to him, the fact that she would try to set me up with the man in charge of my father's funeral completely blows my mind.

"Uh, hey, Gen," he stammers. I haven't really paid attention to him this week, caught in a cloud of grief over everything that's happened recently. He is kind of cute though, in a creepy mortician kind of way. Don't get me wrong, he might be a great guy, but I just can't see myself being the girlfriend or wife of a funeral director. I can barely endure this. I don't know how this guy does it, day in and day out. It must make life seem so fleeting and pointless.

"Hi, Mitch," I say, hoping that the small smile I'm giving him doesn't encourage any romantic thoughts. We talk about unimportant stuff the entire time we're setting up, so I think I'm home free by the time we're done. But, nope, my life doesn't work that way.

"So, um, Gen." Mitch is squirming, actually squirming, as he talks to me.

"Would you like to go grab something to eat sometime?"

Seriously? We're setting things up for my father's funeral and you're asking me to go get dinner? I just stare at him at first and he becomes increasingly uncomfortable. Finally, after a few minutes, I take pity on him, telling him that I can't because I need to be here for my mom and that I just got out of a relationship. "Thank you, but I'm not ready right now."

"Well, if you change your mind, give me a call." He looks crestfallen, which soothes my ego, and hands me his card. I smile at him as he walks away. After he's gone, I suck in a breath of relief.

It'll be funny one day, rational me whispers in my mind, *Remember the time Mom tried to set you up at the funeral?*

And that's why you're locked in a closet, I retort.

Once everything is set up and I've gotten CJ and myself ready to go, Mom and I head for the funeral home. It's the last place I want to be today, and I can't help but wish Daniel was here to help me through this. He's not though, and it's my fault. I'm the one who chose to believe the worst, but he also didn't say anything to defend himself, so I can't decide if my mother was right or not. Why didn't he say something?

When we walk inside, I come to a complete stop at the sight of the casket at the front of the room. The lid is open and I can just barely see my father's folded hands. Mom continues past me just as a hand touches my elbow. Turning, I see Lanie, her eyes red-rimmed from recent tears. She puts her arms around both CJ and me, hugging us tightly and telling me how sorry she is. She releases me, but clutches my hand tightly as we walk up to the front of the room.

At this point, I'm numb to everything going on around me. Certain things catch my attention, but they're meaningless—the scent of the home, the way it smells like lemons, and the ugly pink carpet beneath my feet. This can't be happening. I wish to God this were a cruel joke. I wish Daddy would sit up, smiling, and say he played a prank on us. But it won't happen. The time to bargain with my deaf deity has come and gone.

CJ starts struggling in my arms and saying, "Pops! Pops! Pops! Pops!" over and over again. I didn't think my heart could break further, but watching him try to get to his Pops almost breaks me. I pull him closer to me, murmuring nonsense words in an attempt to keep him calm.

"Here, let me take him," Lanie says quietly, reaching to lift CJ from my arms. I don't want to let him go, but I can't bear listening to him call for his grandfather. He doesn't understand why Pops won't get up and come get him. He keeps calling my dad and every time it drives a nail into my heart.

"Pops is asleep, baby. You'll see him again." I kiss his forehead and hand him to Lanie. CJ goes willingly because he loves Aunt Lanie and her huge-ass earrings. His chubby little hands immediately reach for a hoop. "Thanks, Lanie."

Mom thanks her too and Lanie walks out of the room. The next two hours pass quickly, a blur of faces and condolences until I can't remember any one person who came in. Everyone moves to the chapel for the service. Scanning the crowd, I feel a painful jolt at the sight of Daniel standing at the back of the room, his eyes locked on me. We stare at each other for only a few minutes, before my mom nudges me to keep moving and take my seat.

The service goes by in a blur; I can't tell the title of a single song that was played or any of the words that were said. I sat in my seat, stunned, numb, and mute. We go through the motions like robots and I'm sitting there, thinking too many thoughts, my mind jutting off in too many directions. I think about anything and everything, because I don't want to think about the part where we lower my father into the ground.

I shift my mind to Daniel—I can't believe he came, that he's here. It's strange, especially after the way we parted. I called him a gold-digger and he shows up on one of the worst days of my life with nothing to gain from standing there. I wonder if mom is wrong. How desperate is Daniel to live his own life without his horrible father? Would he really pretend to care about me? Would he show up at a funeral to keep the gig going? That seems beyond cruel, especially after he was outed. So, then, why is he here?

You were wrong. Occam's Razor, dumbass.

God, she's getting pissy. There's a time for logic and there's a time to lock it up and follow your heart.

What do you think I'm telling you to do?

My stomach drops when I realize what I've done. That voice, the one that tells me all these things I've chosen to ignore, wasn't the rational side of me at all. It's my heart. I've locked her up since Cade died and refused to let her out. She's the part of me that let me live and love, laugh and enjoy my life. And now that I've realized it, I have no idea how to let her out again. I don't trust her anymore—that part of me brought me incredible heartache—how can I trust her after that?

Because you're turning into a shell of the woman you should be. You locked your heart away from the world so you wouldn't get hurt again, but it didn't change a damn thing, Genny. You're still hurting.

My heart races because the end is coming. I can't stand and watch them lower him into the ground.

SECOND CHANCES

At the end, everyone gets up to leave, many of them planning to come to our house later. I search the room, trying to find Daniel in the crowd, but I don't see him anywhere. I start pushing through people, intent on finding him. I don't know why or what I'm going to say when I see him, but my gut instinct—the one I've been blocking—is that I made a horrible mistake. As soon as I escape the funeral home, I see him walking toward his truck.

Trying to hurry over, I'm cursing the fact that I wore heels. I'm definitely not coordinated enough to run in them, hell, I can barely walk in them. But, my mother frowned deeply at my flats, so I wore the shoes she picked out instead. Of course, they have three inch heels and it's been raining today, so I'm likely to break my neck before I make it over to him.

By the time I get to his truck, he's shutting the door and like an idiot I grab it, thinking I can stop him. Thankfully, he has better reflexes than I do and manages, barely, to keep the door from shutting on my fingers. He steps out, watching me closely, as I self-consciously pull the cardigan I'm wearing, over my lightweight black sheath dress, tighter around me.

"I'm sorry about your dad, Gen," he says gently, his eyes softening for just a second, gazing down at me sympathetically before they harden again. This new, hardened Daniel causes my heart to clench and my eyes to water. I sniffle and he reaches out to put his arm around me, but catches himself before actually touching me. Pulling back, he takes a step away from me and the small distance feels like an insurmountable chasm.

"Thanks Dan," I say quietly, feeling the sting of his refusal to touch me in any way. His jaw tightens and he nods, suddenly looking anywhere but at me.

Clearing his throat he asks, "Where's CJ?"

"Lanie has him. He kept—" my voice breaks and I take a deep breath before continuing, "CJ was hollering for my dad and didn't understand why he wouldn't get up." Daniel gazes at me when my voice breaks, but he still makes no move to touch me.

SECOND CHANCES

Daniel's eyes are understanding, but still hard, as he stands in front of me, just out of reach. "I'm sure it's hard for him. He's too little to understand all of this." He looks away from me again, his whole body stiff and unyielding. "Well, I guess I better be going. I'm sorry for your loss. Yours and your mom's." He turns slightly, grabbing the door to his truck and pulling it open. "I'll see you around."

Before I even realize I'm doing it, I reach out and grip his wrist, keeping him from getting into the truck. "Wait, Daniel. Can we talk for a few minutes?" My voice pleads with him, but he doesn't say anything at first.

Running his free hand through his hair, he huffs out a breath. "I don't think that's a good idea, Gen." I hate that it's like this. I hate that he's calling me Gen instead of Genevieve. That he doesn't even want to look at me.

"Please, Daniel, I don't want things to end this way." I'm begging now, and completely unashamed. I need to get this off my chest.

He only shakes his head. "I'm sorry, Gen. I just... I can't. I have to go." Then, he hops up in his truck and shuts the door. He doesn't say anything further as he starts the engine, never even looking back as he leaves me standing alone in the parking lot. It's a fairly warm day, but I feel cold. The type of cold that's bone deep and crippling.

Trying my damnedest to keep the tears at bay, I make my way back to the funeral home where my mom stands, glaring at me. She opens her mouth to chastise me, I'm sure, but I put up a hand to stop her. "Not now, Mom." Her mouth snaps shut, her teeth clicking together at the force, but she says nothing. I take my son from her and head for the car, careful not to say anything about what just happened. Today isn't the day for it.

Chapter 16

Over the next three weeks, I try numerous times to reach out to Daniel, sending him text messages and leaving voicemails, but he never responds or calls me back. I'm sure I seem like a stalker, or the creepy ex that just won't leave him alone, but I'm desperate. I need to explain what happened that night. He hasn't been back to mow the lawn either, although I didn't think he would return. My mom told him point blank that he was fired and I didn't correct her.

By the middle of the third week, I'm irate that he's ignoring me. In fact, the last voicemail I left him was pretty harsh.

"Hi, Daniel, it's me, Genevieve…again. I'd appreciate some kind of response, even if it's just to tell me to go to Hell. Thanks."

Okay, so maybe it wasn't that harsh, but I don't understand why he's freezing me out this way. Well, actually I do understand, I just don't like it. The last few weeks have been awful, and I miss him. I miss our talks, dinners, the way he made me laugh, and the way he played with CJ. I loved watching them together. CJ asks for 'da' which kills me even more. I know he means Dan, but does he have to call him da? I've made such a mess of everything and I have no clue how to fix it. He should have said something. Daniel should have defended himself.

What if I was accused of being after him for his money? How would I react?

Pretty much the same—pissed beyond words, because I actually loved him.

Oh shit. I freeze when I realize what I've thought. I loved him. Pressing my eyes together, I pinch my nose and try to avoid the headache that threatens to split my skull in two.

SECOND CHANCES

The doorbell rings and I go let Lanie and Erin in. Maggie wanted to come, but it's her wedding anniversary and she figured she needed to spend the night with Luke. Both girls hug me tightly as they walk by, heading straight for my kitchen with the four bottles of wine Lanie brought with her. When I make it back to the little room, she's already put three of them in the fridge and is in the process of popping the cork on the fourth. Reaching up, I grab three glasses from the cabinet above the sink. I hand them over for her to pour the cheap white wine into.

"So, what are you going to do about Daniel?" After one hour and one and one-half bottle of wine, Lanie sure doesn't pull any punches. I instantly regret spilling my guts the last time she brought drinks to my house. I probably should have learned my lesson.

I shrug. "Nothing. He doesn't want to talk to me. I'm not going to continue to grovel. Maybe I made a mistake, and I know I hurt him, but I can't make him forgive me." I can't seem to stop the verbal avalanche once I start. Wine is pretty much a truth serum for me. I'm such a lightweight. Lanie and Erin drink the majority of the wine, I'm only on my third glass and I'm about to fall over.

"You need to look at it from his point of view," Erin slurs, waving her half-full wine glass around in the air. If I weren't so depressed, I'd be laughing at her obvious drunkenness. She's not much better at holding her alcohol than I am. "He's a guy, Genny! You know how fragile their poor little egos are! You just need to show up at that bar he's working at on the weekends wearing a sexy little outfit. I guarantee he'll listen then!" She starts to slam her wineglass down on the table, but misses it by a mile, sloshing wine all over the floor. "Oops," she mutters, setting it down gently and then almost falling out of her chair when she tries to bend over and wipe the spilled wine off the floor.

I'm not paying attention to what she's doing because I'm fixated on what she just said. "Wait...what bar? What are you talking about? Daniel's working at a bar?" How long has she known about this and why is she just now telling me?

SECOND CHANCES

Lanie claps a hand over Erin's mouth, her eyes suddenly wide. "Uh oh, we weren't supposed to tell you that." Then she whispers, "Shit. Stupid, stupid Lanie." She gives me a guilty look, but doesn't say anything further.

"What bar?" I bite out. "How do you know where he's working, and how long have you guys been keeping it from me?" I narrow my eyes, my anger obvious, even to their drunk asses.

Lanie looks everywhere but at me as she answers my questions. "The Esquire Tavern, we saw him when we went there with Maggie two weekends ago. He asked me not to tell you we saw him."

I'm so mad, I can barely speak. "Lanie, I'm your best friend! How could you keep this a secret? You know how badly I want to talk to him." My wine sits on the coffee table, completely forgotten as I gape at her in disbelief. I can't believe she's been keeping this from me!

Suddenly, I can't sit still any longer, so I get up and start to pace. My mind is spinning so fast I can barely keep up, but her words are bouncing around in my head over and over. I need to see him. I feel like my brain's broken because I think the words over and over again, but it's all I can focus on, the need to see him, to explain, to talk it out.

Lanie and Erin watch me pace, their heads twisting back and forth comically, until I actually see Lanie's skin take on a green tinge. Coming to a stop in front of her, I look down, putting my hands on my hips, and say, "What nights does he work there?"

She shrugs, "I've only seen him on the two Friday nights and once on Saturday." Ugh. If he's only there those nights, that means I have to wait two days before I can see him. "Oh no," she says, her voice suddenly sounding completely sober. "I know that look. What are you going to do?" She leans forward to study me closely, making me want to squirm under her scrutiny.

"Nothing!" I say indignantly. "I'm just going to go talk to him." Chewing on my thumbnail, I give her a pleading glance. "Can you watch CJ Friday night? Please?"

SECOND CHANCES

Lanie shakes her head, her expression slightly pitying. "No, Genny. You need to let this go. If he doesn't want to talk to you, if he isn't interested in forgiving you, you can't force him to. I'm not going to help you get yourself hurt any further. This will make it worse."

I appreciate the sentiment and the fact that she's trying to protect me from myself. I'm positive though that if I can get him to just give me his undivided attention for a few minutes and actually listen to what I have to say, he'd talk to me. Then we could fix things and finally move on from this.

"Guys, I'm finally ready to move on—with him."

Lanie's eyes fill with tears. She springs up, wrapping her arms around me and squeezing me so tight that I feel like my eyes are going to burst from their sockets. "I'm so glad you're ready to move on, Genny! But, maybe you should chalk Daniel up as your rebound guy and find someone else. I mean, it's one thing to fantasize about the younger guy, but is he really who you should try to build a life with?" She pulls back to search my eyes, and whatever she sees there must tell her how I feel about calling Daniel my, "rebound guy".

"That's not what he is Lanie. He brought me back to life. He makes me feel beautiful and capable. He understands me in a way no one has since Cade. I can't help it, that's how I feel. And it makes me feel better that Cade was the one who hired him in the first place—he picked him out. That sounds weird—listen, I mean that Cade thought he had potential, that Daniel was a good guy."

Lanie still looks skeptical. "Yeah, okay... I'm glad he makes you feel that way, but come on Genny! Cade hired Dan-the-kid to mow his grass. He didn't hire Daniel the man to take his place if he was out of the picture."

"You're right," I say, with a sigh. "But, Cade wasn't planning to be out of the picture, Lanie. He trusted Daniel to look after the house while he was gone, and Daniel was a man when Cade was deployed that last time." A memory flashes behind my eyes—Cade and Daniel talking. When I walked into the room, they went silent. I don't think he was raffling me off, I think he was asking Daniel to look after me. Cade asked everyone to look after me, so it wasn't abnormal.

Lanie knows that I'm stubborn when I finally make up my mind about something, so we spend the remainder of the night drinking wine and watching bad television. My mind is half on the matchmaking show we're watching and half on planning exactly how I'm going to approach Daniel on Friday night. Lanie and Erin are both still refusing to watch CJ while I go talk to him, so I've got to figure out how to get my mom to babysit without telling her exactly what I'm planning to do.

Once Lanie is passed out in the guest room, it's just me and Erin left watching this stupid show Daniel introduced me to. She's had just enough wine that when she says, "I really should go on that show," in a completely serious voice, my head swivels around to look at her in shock.

"You should go on *Catfish*? Why?" Not long after Cade died, Erin caught her fiancé doing the dirty with his secretary. She hasn't talked about other men since.

She shrugs, "I've been talking to this guy online for awhile and every time we're supposed to finally meet, something comes up and he has to cancel his plans. I'm betting he's probably either the girl in college who wanted to convert me, or a sixteen-year-old boy that's going to have me taken to jail for indecent liberties, thanks to all the phone-sex we've been having for the past six months."

"What the hell?" I spit out my wine and double over laughing. "Where do you find these people? Good God, and this from the person I'm asking for dating advice." It probably wouldn't be that funny if I wasn't so tipsy, but I have to ask her one more question. "So was the girl hot?"

Erin gives me the stink eye, socking me in the arm hard. "Shut up, it's not like I'm certain he's a chick. We've been talking for a few months. He looks cute in his pictures and he sounds really sexy on the phone. He lives in Colorado, has never been to Texas, and owns his own business. If he were really a girl, it wouldn't be horrible. When I was in college I did some things. Let's just say there's a reason I never said anything about her. I don't plan to start talking about it now."

Holy shit! Is that the reason she hasn't said anything about anyone for the longest time? Because she was messing around with a girl? I think I need to get Erin drunk again, preferably when Maggie and Lanie are around. She'll never be able to tell them no. Then, I realize what she just said. "Erin Michaels, you met a random guy on the internet and wanted to more than friend him." I waggle my eyebrows at her.

"It's not like that, dork! It's just nice to have someone to talk to, and chat with at the end of the day. There's this thing I get when I go to sleep at night, and it's worse if I'm alone." My smile fades into concern. Erin just waves her hand at me. "Don't worry about me. You've been through hell and back. I'm just trying to get by and figure things out. And this guy, he makes me smile. If he were closer I would have met up with him, but he's not." She smiles and looks down at her hands, shrugging. "Like I said, he's probably some sixteen-year-old kid with a deep voice. He can't drive past nine, so I'll never have to worry about him breaking my heart or being an ax murderer. Double score!"

She turns back to the television, obviously finished with this conversation and leaving me gaping at her, unable to find the words. Should I comfort her? Will she think I'm making a move if I give her a hug? I can't believe she never told me any of this. I'm staring at the side of her face as Erin studiously ignores me. So I leave it alone, for tonight at least, and I lean back into the couch to watch television until I doze off.

By the time I stumble to my bedroom after consuming too much wine, I've decided that I'm going to tell my mom the truth... at least the partial truth. I'm going to say that I'm ready to move on, to make a life with someone that isn't Cade. She'll be so happy I'm going "man-hunting" that Daniel won't even cross her mind.

Chapter 17

My aunt, who's been staying with my mother since CJ and I went back to our house, called me first thing this morning, concerned by how poorly Mom is dealing well with things. She asks me to please bring CJ over in an attempt to cheer her up. CJ is amazing. It doesn't matter how sad I am, he can always make me smile. I wonder if Mom's been asking for him.

After getting CJ up and fed we head over to her house. The front door is locked when we arrive, so I use the extra key on my own key ring to get inside. This is the house I grew up in. On a normal day, my dad would have been out in the yard, riding his lawnmower. But the lawn has gone to hell and dad isn't here.

I've been dealing with it by telling myself that it's just for a little while. I'll see him again, and Cade. And wherever they are, they're both happy and looking down on us. I know they're happy. Since I released my heart from its prison, life has gotten easier. A person can't live on logic alone, and what's a life without love? My dad adored me. It grieves me to think of Daniel and the relationship he shares with his father. His scars are a constant reminder of the way things were, and still are, between them. I'm thankful for the time I had with my father, and that he was a good man.

When we walk inside, I call out, "Mom? Are you home?" I know she is since I just talked to my aunt an hour and a half ago, but she doesn't know that.

"In here!" Instead of my mom's voice, it's my Aunt Susie that answers back, and even though it seems strange, I head for the den. The scene inside shocks me. My mother and her sister are very similar people, but today, they couldn't look more

SECOND CHANCES

different. My aunt is dressed to the nines, the type of woman who puts on a pantsuit to go to the supermarket, but my mom—holy crap! My mom is wearing a pair of my father's old sweatpants, the kind with holes in them from the number of times they've been washed, and one of his San Antonio Spurs t-shirts. My dad was not a small man, but my mother is a very small woman. The shirt practically drowns her.

It's probably clearer now the reason I've been living in yoga pants and stained t-shirts. When grief like this comes, everything hurts, even skin. Plus, I wore Cade's shirts for a while, too. I kept them as long as they held his scent. The day I finally donated them to a charity nearly killed me, but I held onto a few things—a favorite sweatshirt, a sweater.

I know exactly how Mom is feeling—losing a husband is a pain that hurts like nothing else. The worst part is that no one can carry you through the grief. You have to get to the other side on your own. Friends and family can be there to prod you along, but they can't make you move.

Today, my mother's clothes say she won't be budged.

I carry CJ to Mom, who hasn't even noticed us. She's staring at the television and not seeing a thing. I know she isn't, and it's not just the glazed look on her face. She's watching a daytime judge show, which she hates because she thinks that discussing your personal business on national TV is disgraceful and demeaning.

"Hey, Mom," I say, leaning over to kiss her cheek. She startles at my voice, finally smiling when she sees CJ reaching for her and hears him babbling.

"Gahgah gahgahgahgahgah," he says.

She takes him out of my arms, hugging him tightly to her chest and placing kisses all over his chubby cheeks. He squeals, excited to see her.

"Hi, Genny," is all she says to me before turning her attention right back to my son. "Hi there, Handsome," she says, the smile clear in her voice as she talks to him. "What are you up to today?"

"Mama mama. Gahhagaah." He jabbers at her as she stares down at him, a small smile playing on her lips.

SECOND CHANCES

"How's she doing?" I ask Aunt Susie in a low voice. She watches my mom for a few minutes longer before getting up and gesturing for me to follow her into the kitchen.

I sit down at the bar while my aunt starts making coffee, moving around the kitchen with a huge amount of nervous energy. "Honestly, Genny, I'm not sure. I mean, you see what she's wearing today. It's the third day in a row she's been dressed like that, she won't leave the house and she does nothing but stare at the TV. I don't know what to do for her, there's no way for me to make this any better."

"I wish I knew how to make this part go faster, but I think she needs it. It's hard, I don't remember much about the months following Cade's death, but I know I was a wreck. Mom and Dad helped. Being here helps, even if it seems like she doesn't care—she does."

Aunt Susie looks thoughtful. "I think letting her spend as much time with CJ as she can muster is a good idea. It gives her something to focus on, and something to look forward to. Look at how happy she is right now, and that was just because she saw him. It's the most emotion I've seen from her all week."

Knowing we can't stay in the kitchen much longer without my mom coming to look for us, we head back into the living room where she's on the floor with CJ, his toys spread out all around them. I love watching my mom with him. With me, she may be a complete control freak, convinced she knows what's best for me, whether it's what I want or not. But with my son, she's the doting grandma. She spoils him rotten and he does no wrong in her eyes.

I sit down on the floor with them, pulling CJ into my lap and cuddling him to my chest. I love the baby scent he still has and take every opportunity to smell him. He's going to grow up so fast, he won't always be my baby who loves to cuddle. CJ grabs my face and squishes my cheeks together, making me have a fish-face.

"Mama!"

"Hwey, waby." He giggles when I try to talk, and my mothers' smile broadens. I grab CJ and roll onto my back, holding him over my head. His arms and legs dangle down, swatting at me, as he giggles. Then a big glob of drool falls on my face. Laughing, I put him down. "Cheater."

My mom watches us together, a soft look in her eyes. CJ crawls over to her and they snuggle and he gets her to giggle softly.

Deciding that it'd be good for her to have something to do, I ask, "Can you come over and watch CJ tomorrow night?"

"What's tomorrow night? Do you have a date?" She's instantly alert, ready for me to tell her that I've met the perfect man, preferably older than me, rich, with a stable career. Little does she know that young, not so rich, with a new business is more my type.

Shaking my head, I tell her, "No, no date. Just going out to a bar over on the River-walk." I leave it at that, not wanting to lie to her, but not wanting to get into the details either.

"Oh," she says, her disappointment clear. It doesn't stop her for long though. "I'd love to spend some time with my grandson. And, if I come to your house, you won't even have to come home!" Jeez, she's offering to babysit while I go out for a one-night stand? Always classy, mom.

"Mom!" I gape at her, my face flaming red. Aunt Susie laughs.

"Well, a little sex now and then never killed anyone."

Aunt Susie nearly chokes. "Stop encouraging your daughter into whoredom."

"Is that a town? If it is Lanie will want directions," I say. Mom gently slaps me on the back of my head, but she's laughing.

"Lanie's a good girl, she just doesn't know it."

"Good girls don't have one-night stands, Ma."

She cringes. "Mother or Mom, please. And I never said you weren't a good girl, I just said that a little loving might take the edge off, so don't hurry home." With that, she goes back to ignoring me and coos at CJ. I glance at Aunt Susie who looks like she's thinking we should institutionalize mom in a designer straight jacket.

"Uh, thanks Mom. I probably won't need you to babysit overnight, although you're welcome to the guest bedroom if you want. That way you won't have to drive home late."

"You better not stay out late," Aunt Susie chides, which makes my mother come to life. No one scolds me, except her. She and her sister snap back and forth while she plays with the baby.

I stay at my mom's until late afternoon. When CJ falls asleep, my mom prods, "Please go shopping. I love this workout, lesbian look you have going on, but I think it's time to buy a new dress. Go out. I'll watch CJ."

Erin's words about wearing a sexy dress come back to me and I think about what I'm going to wear tomorrow night. When I refused to accept it, Mom returned my birthday dress. I don't own a sexy dress. "Really?" I ask, not wanting to make things harder for her.

Mom's jaw drops as her eyebrows go way up into her hairline. "You're seriously thinking about it? Go! Don't let me stop you. Aunt Susie and I can take care of CJ. Take your time. Buy some nice panties too."

"Mom!"

Aunt Susie pinches her nose. "Oh, dear God."

"You only live once. Make it count." Mom takes my hand, squeezes it and says, "Go on. Get out of here." I hug her and say thank you. I have a dress to buy.

Chapter 18

My mom arrives early to babysit CJ. She shows up just after I get out of the shower. I took extra time to make sure that all the pertinent areas are shaved and exfoliated because I want my skin to be soft to the touch. I'm choosing to be optimistic, hoping that we'll talk and maybe we'll have some making up to do. I meant it when I told Lanie and Erin that I'm ready to move on with him.

"Hi, Genny," she says, leaning in to hug me and give me a kiss on the cheek. She's actually been a lot mellower for the past few weeks. It's like losing dad made her realize that her life isn't the way she wanted and she's changing things, at least she's trying. Her outfit is confused. It's her dress slacks and Daddy's sweatshirt, and it swallows her down to her knees. I glance at her feet and she's wearing stockings with patent leather shoes. Aunt Susie must have had a stroke when she saw mom leave the house.

"Hey, Mom." I hug her before stepping back to let her inside. As she looks around my freshly painted foyer, painted the same color as my also freshly painted dining room, her eyes come to rest on me standing in only a towel with my hair dripping down my chest.

Her eyes scan me quickly. "Do you always answer the door wearing nothing but a towel? Some men might take that as an invitation."

"Good thing you weren't the UPS man, then." I smile at her.

"Maybe."

My eyes widen. "Mom! Stop being all vixen-like. I can't handle it. Besides, I knew it was you. I saw your car out front." Holding the knot that's keeping my towel from showing all my assets, I narrow my eyes at her. "I need to get dressed. I'm not going to the bar in a towel."

"It would send a clear message." She's smirking, teasing me.

"I don't think I want to project 'crazy mess' much further than the doormat, Ma." She cringes at the use of 'ma.' She smiles at me, knowing I did it on purpose. "CJ's in his crib if you want to go get him."

I pad up the stairs with Mom at my heels. She takes a turn into CJ's room and I head into mine. My heart is racing a little bit. This is crazy. The man doesn't want to talk to me, but I can't get past the feeling that I made a mistake. I study the dress I've chosen to win Daniel back. It's an emerald green vintage-style dress with a diamond cut neck that I found at a shop on the River-walk that specializes in pinup style dresses. It shows just a little bit of cleavage, and it's in the classy style that I love. I've paired it with cream-colored peep toe heels that are higher than I'm used to, especially considering the fact that I've been living mainly in flip flops and sneakers for the past two years. I really hope I don't break my ankle, although the shoes make my legs look really nice.

I leave my hair down, letting it fall in waves just below my shoulders because the green in the dress brings out the red tones in my dark hair. I keep most of my makeup light, but take time with my eyes, making sure my liner and mascara are perfect. Aside from the butterflies threatening to fly out my nose, I think I'm ready to go. I've spent two days planning what I'm going to say and how the night is going to go. I don't think I can be any better prepared.

Pressing a hand to my stomach, trying to calm my nerves. I pick up the matching purse I bought this afternoon and head for the stairs, hoping my mom doesn't ask too many questions about what I'm doing tonight. I don't want to outright lie to her, but I also don't want to fight with her about Daniel. She's made me feel bad enough about the feelings I have for him.

My mother is focused on CJ when I walk into the living room, babbling all kinds of nonsense to him as they sit together on the floor with his toys spread out around them. Concentrating on not falling over, I bend over to place a kiss on the top of his head, smoothing down his pale blonde hair.

"Oh, Genevieve, you look just beautiful!" my mom gushes as she looks me over, head to toe. "Do you have a specific man in mind tonight? Or are you girls just hoping to meet some new men?" She's entirely too excited at the prospect of me dating.

I have to be very careful to be truthful without letting her know that I'm going out alone, and to see a very specific guy. "There's a specific guy, but I don't want to jinx it Mom. We'll see how it goes, okay?" I bend to kiss her cheek before hightailing out of the house to avoid any further questions.

When I shut the door to my car, I let out a sigh of relief. I hate lying and being deceitful, but I really don't want her destroying the confidence I've spent the last two days building up. Putting myself out there isn't going to be easy, but I have to try.

Pulling into the closest lot to the bar, I put the car in park and take a deep breath. I can do this. He will talk to me, and we will talk. He'll tell me Mom was wrong. I know he will. Looking in the mirror on my visor, I make sure my makeup is all still in place and squeeze my eyes shut tightly, trying to psych myself up for what I'm about to do.

Walking into the bar, I don't immediately see Daniel and I worry that maybe Lanie was wrong, or that he's off tonight. The place is packed because it's forties night. Big Band music is blaring and a ton of people bounce around the room, dancing in ways that I thought no one knew anymore. I stop and stare for a moment. A man with dark hair and strong arms swings a girl around his waist. Nimbly, she floats to the floor like a falling petal, slips between his legs and jumps up again—the smile on her face is huge. Brown hair clings to her sweaty forehead and I envy her for a second. They look so happy together, so normal. His white shirt clings to his back. They must have been dancing for hours.

Pushing through the throng of people, I take the last empty seat at the bar and look around, hoping he's here, that I didn't make this trip for nothing. I almost sag in

SECOND CHANCES

relief when he comes out from what must be a back room, carrying a case in his arms.

It's as if he can sense me here, his head jerks up and his eyes meet mine. His are unreadable; I can't tell how he feels about seeing me at first. It's pretty obvious though when he shakes his head and looks away from me, his jaw tight in irritation. Deflating slightly, I order a glass of wine to avoid being told to move along and let a paying customer take my seat.

I already know my alcohol tolerance is low, so when I see him watching me from the other end of the bar I raise the glass up to my lips and take a minuscule sip. As soon as he turns to another customer, I dump the glass in the plant next to the end of the bar. It gets me some weird looks from the people around me, but I studiously ignore them and order another drink.

As much as Daniel is trying to ignore me, I see him sneak looks at me on and off for the next ten minutes. During that time, I've gotten a vodka cranberry, which I've only taken about three sips from and am already starting to feel lightheaded. That's probably why dumping the rest of the drink in the napkin holder seems like a smart idea.

The rest of the night goes like that—I pretend that I don't see Daniel pretending to completely ignore me, while I order drinks back to back. In addition to dumping my drink in the plant and the napkin holder, I also dumped almost half a glass into the bowl of peanuts sitting between me and the blonde man sitting beside me. He doesn't notice, or at least I don't think he does.

A guy tries to talk to me. He's all smiles. "Hey, gorgeous. Can I buy you a drink?"

"But where would I put it?" I try not to laugh. I'm seriously running out of places to dump drinks.

His dark brows lift and I must have set off his crazy chick alarm, because he excuses himself quickly.

I order one last drink, vodka neat, intending to swallow the whole thing this time. I stare at the little glass and pick it up, ready to throw it back, but I lose my nerve once the liquid slips over my lips. Glancing around the room, panicked, I look for a place to spit out the drink. Fuck, this is like drinking fire! I try not to draw attention to myself, but I can't swallow it. The longer I hold the liquor in my mouth, the more it burns. I open my brand new purse and spew. Liquor sprays in along with a massive amount of drool, ruining my wallet, my lipstick, and, of course, my cell phone.

That's when I notice Swing Dance Man standing next to me with one dark eyebrow raised far into his hairline.

"That's one way to do it," he says, smiling. There's a dimple in his cheek. The woman he was dancing with rushes up behind him. Fuckbunnies! He noticed. My face flames in embarrassment. I guess I wasn't as stealthy as I thought.

"This was a great idea Peter! The band is amazing!" She pushes her wall of curls back and asks, "Did you order the drinks? I'm so thirsty I could die."

Peter nods and hands her a glass. She turns and bounces away into the crowd, dancing as she goes. He glances at me with sympathy, maybe even empathy—like he's been there.

Staring at the bar, I utter, "Don't feel sorry for me." I don't know where the words come from, but I don't want his pity.

"I wouldn't dream of it." The sincerity in his voice rings true. "It's just that, well, I recognize a kindred spirit when I see one. We've been through Hell and back. Am I right?" I look into his dark blue eyes, too afraid to answer.

He drops his gaze to his drink and then tips his head to the side, slipping his fingers through his dark hair. "You're a survivor. Don't give up." He smiles crookedly before walking away, and disappearing into the crowd.

I stop paying attention, which is obviously a bad idea because only a few seconds later, Daniel is finally standing in front of me. "What the hell are you doing, Genevieve?" His voice is low, almost gravelly.

"What do you mean?" I ask, giving him what I hope is an innocent look, but that probably looks more like I'm having some weird kind of seizure.

He glares at me, his hands folded over his chest and looking very unwelcoming.

SECOND CHANCES

"Do you really want me to tell you all about how I saw you dumping your drinks and what I watched you dump them into?"

"No" I stutter, mortified. Why did I think dumping the drinks would be a good idea? Oh yeah, I thought that if he thought I was on a mission to get drunk he might come over and talk to me. Remembering suddenly that talking was the whole reason I came here tonight, I draw myself up so that my spine is straight and look him in the eyes.

"Daniel, can we please talk? I have so much I need to say to you." I know the look on my face now is pleading for him to give me a chance, but I've had just enough alcohol to not care how desperate I look. I need him to know how much I regret the way I acted that night. Or, I guess more accurately, the way I didn't react. I was wrong and I need to tell him.

Pinching the bridge of his nose, Daniel says nothing at first. Finally, he heaves a heavy sigh and meets my gaze once more. "Gen," he begins, and I know by the tone of his voice exactly what he's getting ready to say. It doesn't stop the pain that rips through my chest when he finally says it though. "I think you should go. I don't think we have anything left to say to each other."

Realizing he's never going to forgive me for not having faith in him, I accept defeat, gather my things, and head for the door. I walk as fast as my unsteady legs can carry me. I will not cry. The last thing I want now is for him to know how much refusing to even let me explain hurts. It wasn't easy for me to come here tonight, not that he seems to care. When I finally make it through the crowd of people and out into the cooler air, I lean against the wall, tipping my head back and trying to compose myself.

Chapter 19

Completely dejected over the fact that Daniel still won't let me explain, I slowly walk back to the parking lot. After tripping over every single crack in the sidewalk, I'm regretting wearing these shoes with every step. Honestly, if I weren't worried about stepping on glass, I'd just take them off and walk barefoot.

The walk back to my car gives me time to pound the pavement and work out my anger issues. How long has it been since I made an attempt to reach out to a guy? I risked my heart and got slammed down. I knew it was a possibility, but Daniel was worth the risk. If I hadn't done this I would have spent the rest of my life wondering if there was anything else I could have done to patch things up with him. Now I know. It's over. He won't forgive me, and the more I think about it, the more I know my mother was wrong. I'm a dumb ass. Daniel always paid for everything. He wasn't a leech, mooching off of me at all. He's not a gold-digger, and when he needed me to have a little faith in him, I had none.

The truth is, I suck. I'm not good at this, or at life. Too many people I love have ended up in the ground too quickly and I'm mad. It wasn't supposed to be this way, and then when I find someone, I screw that up too. I'm not going to be a victim anymore. This is never happening again.

When I reach into my sodden bag for what I'm sure will be dripping car keys, I find that they're no longer in my purse. Shit. I'm trying to remember where I last saw my keys, but the only thing I remember is dropping them on the ground when I got out of the car. Dammit. I don't think I even picked them up. I was in too much of a hurry to get inside and see Daniel.

SECOND CHANCES

As I walk up to where I parked my car, I see someone getting into it. Seriously? I stand there, jaw dropped, and stare. I've had it. Something inside of me snaps and I race over to the driver's side, jerk the door open, and see a kid who can't even be old enough to drink. He's staring up at me in shock. Before he can react, I scream, "Get out of my car!" Grabbing him by the arm, I start trying to drag him out while beating the shit out of him with my purse. I'm like a ninja when I'm pissed. Bag to face, finger to eye, knee to nuts, plus lots of screaming. I don't even know what I'm saying anymore, but the kid is laying half in and half out of my car.

I continue to girlie-slap him until he's had enough. Jerking out of my grasp, he shoves me away from him with both hands, causing me to stumble back and fall. He rights himself in the seat. I land hard on my bottom, putting my hands out behind me to break my fall and scraping my palms against the rough asphalt. The pain doesn't really register, because the kid gets out of the car to stand over me menacingly. I realize now that attempting to beat the shit out of a car thief who outweighs me by at least forty pounds wasn't such a stellar plan.

Looking up at the guy, I tremble as his lip curls into a snarl. My heart is racing and I'm sitting on the ground, scared and unable to move. His hand darts out, grabbing my arm and yanking me up so that I'm standing in front of him. The hateful look on his face has me shaking and I squeeze my eyes shut in terror, screaming in his face. I don't want to see whatever's coming next.

When his hand suddenly vanishes and I hear a grunt of pain, my eyes fly open. Daniel is holding the guy by the throat and looks pissed. They're staring at each other, both of them livid. The car thief is gripping both of Daniel's wrists, trying to remove them from his throat.

Daniel leans in close to him and snarls, "Don't you fucking touch her." The car thief's eyes widen a second before Daniel's fist clocks him in the side of the head, snapping it to the side. Releasing him, Daniel steps back, waiting to see what the kid is going to do. The thief turns back to him, his eyes wild and unfocused. Daniel doesn't back down, instead he glares back at him, ready for a fight.

When the thief lunges, Daniel punches him in the face. Something cracks, someone yelps, but it's mostly swinging arms and a lot of swearing. That is, until Daniel knocks the thief down. I think it's over, but the other guy doesn't stop. He trips Daniel and now they're rolling around on the ground beating the shit out of each other. I'm scared to death that the thief has a gun. I don't want anyone to get shot. I look around for something to club him with, but the only thing I can find is a wire hanger. I hover, not knowing what to do, hanger in one hand, purse in the other.

Finally, Daniel's fist hits him hard one last time. They're on their knees when blood goes flying from the thief's mouth as his face collides with the pavement. He skids to a stop and doesn't move. Daniel stands and stares down at the guy for a second, his eyes still burning with anger. When the thief doesn't move, he turns to look at me.

Daniel walks over and takes hold of my arms, studying me. "Are you okay?" Unable to speak, I nod once, staring up at him in awe. He starts checking me over for injuries, brushing the loose gravel off my hands and seeing my blood. "The fucker hurt you."

"It's just my hands. Don't!" I tug Dan's arm when he looks like he's ready to go back and bury the guy. "Please, don't. I'm okay."

"Are you hurt anywhere else? God, Gen, I went out back to breakdown some boxes and I hear you screaming at the top of your lungs. I couldn't run fast enough. I thought I was too late." His brow is covered in sweat and grime. His once white shirt is torn and his elbow is bleeding.

I shake my head before finally remembering how to speak. "I'm okay, really. My butt is a little sore from falling, but other than that I'm okay." I look up at him, wanting to say so many things, but I know he doesn't want to hear it, so I press my lips together.

"Good," Daniel nods, satisfied with my answer. "I'm sorry about your dress." Looking down, I see that my brand new dress, the one I was sure Daniel would notice me in, has a big rip up the hip. It goes almost to the bottom of my panties.

"It's not your fault," I tell him, my voice trembling. The adrenaline boost from the night is wearing off and I know I'm going to break down soon. I feel it coming. "Um, thanks for the rescue. I guess I should get home."

Daniel stares at me in disbelief. "Go home? Genevieve, you need to call the police. That guy was trying to steal your car, and if I hadn't walked up when I did, who knows what else he would have done to you."

"I just want to go home and forget tonight ever happened." Between the terror and Daniel refusing me, I feel completely drained and I want nothing more than to go to bed and pretend this entire night was a bad dream.

Gripping my chin in his hand, Daniel tips my head up so he can look into my eyes. "Genevieve, you can't just forget this happened. This guy," he points over to where the thief is lying unconscious on the ground, "shouldn't get to walk away from this. Not only was he trying to steal your car, he hurt you. There's no way in hell he's getting away with that!"

I'm falling apart. I can't control my words no matter how hard I try. Lashing out, I spew, "Why not? You did."

Daniel's jaw tightens. "That's not fair. You hurt me too, Genevieve." He holds his hand out in front of him. "Give me your phone," he orders.

"You seem a little preoccupied for someone who doesn't care about me."

"Cut it out, Gen." Daniel narrows his eyes at me. "Don't make me come and get it."

I smile. "Yeah, I knew you wanted some. Come and get it."

"Gen."

"Dan."

"Call the fucking cops."

"I don't feel like fucking."

"He's going to wake up!" Daniel's hands are flailing. He looks like a lost Muppet.

"So, hit him again. Don't let him talk. You're good at that."

SECOND CHANCES

"Are you fucking kidding me? I tried to talk, you were the one who didn't listen, so don't give me that shit."

"Do you kiss your mother with that mouth?" I realize what I've said, but it's too late. I should have just kicked him in the nuts. "I'm sorry. I didn't mean it like that." I hand him the phone.

Daniel ignores my verbal land-mine and plays with the phone for a minute, pushing buttons and trying to turn it on, but nothing happens.

"Um, it's probably not going to work." Daniel's questioning gaze meets mine and I look away, embarrassed about what I'm getting ready to say. "It was in my purse when I...uh..." Cringing, I say the rest so fast that the words all run together, "got it wet."

"Genevieve," Daniel groans in exasperation.

"Daniel," I mimic.

"How'd it get wet?"

"You already know. I kind of put one of my drinks in there."

"Why would you pour a drink into your purse?" He's trying hard not to smile, and suddenly so am I.

Shaking my head I tell him, "It was more like spewed, not poured, and there's no way I'm answering that." This whole conversation is completely ridiculous.

"Right," he mutters. "Come on, we'll call from inside the bar. At least there, we can wash the dirt off your hands and you'll be able to sit down while we wait for the police." He puts a hand on the small of my back, gesturing for me to walk in front of him so the tear in my dress isn't as noticeable.

"I can't."

"You have to call the cops."

"That's not what I mean. I can't walk the whole way again, not in these shoes. I can barely stand." He smiles at me. "I'm not sexy. I can only do sneakers and yoga pants."

He sighs and threads his arm around me, letting me lean on him. We start to walk and he says, "Some guys think yoga pants are hot."

SECOND CHANCES

"Really?" I think he's being nice, but on the way back to the bar he explains to me why men love yoga pants, from the tight fitting ass, to the unfashionably sexy camel toe. "So, they're not like sweatpants?"

He laughs. "No, not even close."

When we walk inside, Daniel leads me back to the bar, pulling out a stool for me before walking away. Nice. I made a fool out of myself trying to get him to talk to me, my car was almost stolen, I ripped a dress that cost me over two hundred bucks, we discussed camel toes, and then he sits me down and leaves.

A few people glance at me. I avoid their stares and resist the urge to bury my face in my arms and go to sleep on the table. Suddenly my head feels like it's made of lead. I'm going to sob and pass out. I'm so spaced that I don't notice Dan's back until he starts wiping my hands with a wet cloth, removing all the dirt.

He kneels in front of me. "I called for you."

"Thank you." Our eyes lock as he holds the cold cloth on my hand. I don't want him to leave.

"No problem." He's careful and dabs the cloth to my other hand. Before we say more, the police arrive and I give my statement, telling them about the fair haired guy who tried to steal my car, and how I kinda sorta picked a fight with him.

"Excuse me? Can you explain that?" The cop is older, his shaggy eyebrow lifts slightly.

I shrug. "I had a bad night and I didn't want to—" I sigh, and look him in the eye. "It was stupid, but I didn't want to let him take my car. So I beat him up a little bit, then he punched me. I fell on my butt and screamed. Daniel saved me. The guy was going to hurt me."

Daniel continues to watch me like he's waiting for me to have some sort of mental breakdown, but I'm too lost in my head for that. By the time the cops are done with their questions, it's later than I expected. I'm sure my mother thinks I'm in bed boinking some random guy.

SECOND CHANCES

"Come on, Genevieve," Daniel says quietly, curling his hand around my elbow to help me up. "Let me take you home." I don't protest, instead letting him lead me out of the bar and over to his truck, the same truck I miss seeing parked outside of my house. He opens the door before helping me climb up and heading over to his side.

"I'm sorry. For this, for everything." I don't look at him. I can't. I wrap my arms around my middle and stare straight ahead.

"None of this is your fault."

I shake my head back and forth. "Not just with this, with everything. I'm sorry. You have no idea." Putting a hand over my mouth, I attempt to keep the sudden sobs inside.

Suddenly, tears are streaming down my cheeks and Daniel's arms are wrapped around me. He tucks me closer into him after sliding across the truck's bench seat and murmurs, "Shh, baby. Please don't cry."

I allow myself the comfort of his arms for just a minute before pushing him away from me. "You can stop acting concerned about me now," I say softly. "I'll be fine."

"Damn it, Genevieve!" His voice is loud in the small space and I jump when he smacks the steering wheel with both hands. "Why do you always believe the worst? You believed the worst about me. What happened to the woman who was so strong she didn't want anyone to help her because she could do it all?"

His words slice me open. Every single insecurity I've ever had bubbles to the surface and once I start, I can't stop the words that are pouring out of my mouth. "Strong? I haven't been strong in so damn long. I'm coming loose at the seams and breaking apart. My life has been so lonely for the past two years. My parents and friends are great, but I relied so heavily on my husband that I don't know how to ask anyone else for help. When he was alive, I didn't need to ask anyone for help because he always knew when I needed it. It's so hard to go from that to not knowing who you can count on. I didn't even know how to ask."

"You don't have to do everything on your own! Fuck, Gen, I've been at your house a couple times a week for those two years and you never once asked for help. I had to force you to take a break when CJ was sick, and even then you fought me on it." His hands clench into fists as he turns to stare out the windshield, his jaw tight. "And then, after everything, all the time we spent together, I find out you never trusted me. You thought I was going through your mail and looking at your bank accounts. Shit, Gen. That's damning and there's no pretty way to say it. You either trust me or you don't, and you clearly did not."

My mouth drops open. "I did trust you! I trusted you to help me, I let you in when I wouldn't let anyone else near me."

"Bullshit." He turns to face me, his heated gaze pinning me in my seat. "If you trusted me at all, you would've defended me when your mother accused me of being after your money. Dammit, Genevieve, you know me better than that! After all the time I spent at your house, all the hours we spent talking, and you honestly believed I would use you that way?"

By the end of his tirade, his voice is devoid of anger and just sounds sad. I realize then just how much I hurt him by not immediately defending him. "I don't need your money, Gen," he continues, his shoulders slumped slightly. "I have plenty of my own. My father may hate the idea that I'm not following him into his business, but my grandparents left trust funds for both Melody and me. I'm not hurting for money at all. In fact, I could decide tomorrow that I didn't want to work at all and I could still live comfortably for a long time."

I stare at him, shocked speechless at his confession. When I finally find my voice, the only thing I can say is, "I'm so sorry, Daniel." Closing my eyes tightly, I confess, my own voice barely audible, "I know you wouldn't use me the way my mother suggested, but I was scared. I was so scared of the feelings I have for you, that I let her make me feel like what we were doing was wrong. You don't know how much I regret letting you think I believed her, because I didn't. I just didn't say it. Even though I couldn't admit it to myself—I love you. It scares me. I didn't mean for it to happen, it just did, and I can't do it again. I can't lose someone else, especially not you."

SECOND CHANCES

His hand cups my cheek, and I open my eyes to see his dark blue ones staring at me like he's never seen me before. One side of his mouth tips up and the tightness in his jaw is gone. He looks so relieved. "You love me?"

My eyes dart to the side, not wanting to admit it again. "Don't make me say it again."

Daniel's lifts my chin and drops his head. His mouth is hovering just over mine. I feel his warm breath on my lips as he speaks. "Why not?"

"Because, if you don't feel that way, it's just cruel."

He strokes my hair, pushing a piece behind my ear and cradling my chin so I can't look away. "What if I do feel the same way? What if I love you?" He smiles softly, unsure of my response.

"You love me?" I ask, shocked.

He nods, smiling. "More than anything. Will you forgive me? I should have let you talk, we should have talked this out and I ran like a scared kid. I'm sorry, Gen. I had no idea how you felt."

I squeak out, "Yes," just before his lips touch mine and I'm lost. My hands fly up to grip his shoulders while he moves his hands away from my face to grip my hips and pull me closer to him. When I feel his tongue trace the seam of my lips, I part my own with a sigh, letting him inside so our tongues can tangle together.

Making out in a car like teenagers is definitely overrated. It's obviously been a long time since I've done it, and it's a lot harder now than it used to be. His truck isn't small by any means, but maneuvering so that I can press my body against his isn't easy. I'm up on my knees while he's turned slightly to face me. If it wasn't for the steering wheel, I'd be straddling his lap.

Daniel groans in frustration as he tears his mouth away from mine to say, "I want you more than I've ever wanted anything, Genevieve. Will you come home with me?"

I nod eagerly, desperate to be as close to him as possible. He leans in to kiss me once more, his large hand on my back pressing me closer against him as he takes my mouth aggressively. I've never been kissed like this. Daniel kisses me like it's

SECOND CHANCES

more important than breathing, and I feel the same way. I'm giddy with anticipation of what's going to happen when we get back to his place.

Pulling away from me, Daniel turns to place his shaking hands on the steering wheel, taking a deep breath before he puts the truck in drive. He doesn't say much on the ride to his house, but we don't need words, we both know what's coming next.

Chapter 20

We barely make it into his apartment before he pushes me up against the wall, caging me in with his arms on either side of my head. He towers over me, making me feel as if he can protect me from anything. Heart racing fast, my hands lie flat against the wall by my sides, trembling.

I want this more than anything, but now that I'm here, I'm terrified. Aside from only having sex with one other man, I've had a baby since the last time I had sex. My body was young, my muscles were firm and my skin was unscarred. Now I'm a nervous wreck and there's nothing firm or unscarred, not anymore. Every flaw I have

SECOND CHANCES

is glittering like a disco ball. I wanted to be perfect for him, but my diet and exercise plan went the way of the taco.

Mmmm. Tacos.

No wonder I have mommy thighs. We're about to have sex and I'm thinking about tacos and cursing my big butt. Daniel's lips pass over my throat in the perfect spot and I whimper. All thoughts of food and thighs vaporize.

"Hey," he whispers, after pressing his lips to my neck again and again, making me hotter and more lightheaded. "Whatever you're thinking, stop." Daniel says the last part looking me in the eye, and then trails his knuckles down my cheek, continuing to my neck. There's no way he doesn't feel the rapid fluttering of my pulse. He kisses my neck and lingers, moving slowly back up to my cheek, and then pecks my lips. When he backs away, his blue eyes wash over me, making me gasp for air. I see what he's thinking, what he wants from me and I'm so nervous and excited. The only thing I know for certain is that I want to run, either straight into him or away from him.

Daniel speaks into my ear, his warm breath making my back arch and I try to clutch the wall. "We don't have to do anything, Gen. I'll wait until you're ready. I'll wait forever for you." He kisses my cheek and pulls away, watching me, and smiling softly. "I'm fine with things like this. Kissing you is like breathing in sunshine—it's amazingly hot and fills me from head to toe. I feel like I can fly when I'm with you, Genevieve. There's no rush."

Meeting his gaze, I push him back and he drops his hands to his sides. He probably thinks it's because I'm not ready, but that's not it. His words freed me. My guilt is gone and any hesitation I had flies away. My lips tug into a sexy smile. "Rushing into things sounds kind of nice, though, doesn't it?" Keeping my eyes on his, I reach for the hem of my dress, lifting it up and over my head in one motion. My stomach flips as I toss it to the floor and stand there, letting his gaze rake over me.

I take a deep breath and turn toward him, wearing only my champagne-colored bra, matching panties and heels. I have no idea what he thinks at first, but the way his

SECOND CHANCES

mouth forms a tiny O, the way he drinks me in makes me feel so alive, so sexual. I haven't had anyone look at me this way in a very long time. A giggle bursts through my lips.

"You are…" His voice is breathy, like all the air has been crushed from his lungs. Daniel's eyes travel down my body like a tender caress. His gaze lingers first on the swell of my chest, then on the apex of my thighs, and finally wanders lazily down the entire length of my legs. His heated gaze moves back up my body, before settling on my face. I can barely breathe while he looks me over. "Damn, you're beautiful!" His hands fist at his sides, as if it's taking all of his self-control not to strip me naked and jump me.

The thought makes me smile. Cowboys aren't my thing, but I wouldn't mind being ridden right about now. My lips part as I step closer, so that my chest brushes against his. The response is instant. He gasps and holds onto me while I run my hands up his chest and wrap my arms around his neck. His hands come up to grip my hips, barely touching my skin. The heat of his hands feels like a brand as I pull his head down to touch my lips to his.

Between kisses, I whisper against his mouth, "I want you, Daniel."

His grip on me tightens at the words, as he melds our bodies together. His mouth moves over mine forcefully and he sweeps his tongue past my lips. This is a side of him that I've never seen before, and I'm reveling in his possession, the way he moves me and holds me—as if I'm his and always will be. Holding onto my hips while he continues the kiss, he walks backward, leading me over to the brown leather couch. It's against the wall a few steps away. Taking a seat he pulls me down, so I'm straddling his thighs.

He kisses a trail across my jaw before moving his hot lips down my throat. I tip my head to the side as he reaches a spot just below my ear that makes me quiver. I gasp loudly and start to go limp in his arms, but I fight it.

"Let go, baby," he urges me to give in to that feeling, but it frightens me. I don't know what he's like in bed or what he'll want from me. It makes it exciting, but it scares me too. I want to be at least a little coherent, so I fight the lust that's trying to consume the rest of my mind. It's as if he knows, because he says, "I love you, Genevieve. I won't hurt you, baby." He tips my head and looks into my eyes. "Do you trust me?"

I'm smiling like a fool. "You love me?" He nods and kisses the tip of my nose, and then smiles at me, bashfully. "I love you, too."

He smiles harder. "That is a very good thing."

I kiss the tip of his nose and make a decision—one that makes my heart pound so loudly that I swear he can hear it. The smile fades from my lips as I whisper, "I trust you."

Daniel holds me tight, pressing his body to mine and drops his mouth to my neck once more. When he finds that spot and feels my reaction, he concentrates all of his attention there, stroking his tongue firmly, nipping, and sucking lightly until I surrender every ounce of control with a breathy moan. I'm a puddle in his arms, a sexy doll that he can play with as he pleases.

I can't think anymore; I can only feel. Every inch of my skin is tingling, craving his touch. The spot between my legs is on fire. I want him there and I've lost any discretion I might have had, so I say how much I want him, where I want him, and how I want him.

Daniel gasps every time I say something, begging for him to take me. I want to feel every inch of him and I don't hold back. Every thought, every desire spills over my lips and makes him devour me all the more.

Daniel's hands slide up and down my back, leaving a trail of heat in their wake. The feel of his palms cradling me and the wet heat from his mouth is my undoing. I grind my hips against his, wishing we were closer.

The fact that he's still wearing his fitted grey t-shirt and dark washed jeans while I'm almost naked is like an aphrodisiac. I feel like someone else, bold and sexy, as my fingers tangle in his hair and I pull him back to my lips. His mouth leaves a damp trail down my neck as he kisses from my ear to the spot where my pulse gallops. He groans

SECOND CHANCES

low in his throat before moving his mouth lower, nibbling at my collarbone, and tracing the skin just above the cups of my bra with the tip of his tongue.

Arching my back, I bring my breasts closer to his mouth and feel his fingers working the clasp. The straps slide down my arms and leave me completely bare from the waist up. "Damn," he mutters, "you're perfect, these are perfect." My face heats and I know I'm blushing to the tips of my toes when he takes me into his mouth and sucks... hard. I lose all coherent thought as every feeling in my body centers around the way he's making me feel and the pull of his mouth on my sensitive flesh. He gives my other breast the same treatment, but this time he bites down gently—slowly grazing my skin with his teeth—which makes me cry out. When I arch my back and press into him, Daniel thrusts his hips up against mine, teasing me.

Bringing my hands down to the hem of his shirt, I start pulling it up, desperate to feel his bare skin against mine. He releases me to help, pulling his shirt up and over his head and revealing his tan chest and lickable abs. Daniel laughs, saying, "If you keep looking at me like that, this is going to be over in about three seconds."

My eyes fly up to meet his, and the heat in them sets me on fire. "I'm okay with that."

Daniel groans before placing his hands on my hips, slipping them down to my butt and standing abruptly. His actions leave me no choice but to wrap my legs around his waist. I'm still wearing my heels, but when I try to toe them off, he grips my butt harder.

"Don't. Leave them on," he commands. A thrill shoots through me.

He walks us into his room and lays me down on his bed, before covering me with his body. He presses a kiss to my nose, which makes me smile before he does more. "Keep going?" I nod. "Because we're passing the point of no return. You're too beautiful, and I've wanted you so much for so long. Gen, I don't think I could stop if you asked me—"

Slamming my lips down on his, I silence him with a kiss. It's all the affirmation he needs. Things become hotter with each passing moment and I love the

SECOND CHANCES

feeling of being his, feeling him want me so badly he can't control himself.

Taking my legs, he moves them so that they're cradling his hips. Daniel pushes the bulge behind his zipper against my panty-covered core and I whimper. I manage to grab hold of him, scratching my nails into his shoulder, before he pulls back. Holding himself up with one arm, he trails his other hand down my throat and between my breasts, not stopping until he comes to the silky barrier. He traces the line across my stomach before pushing up so that he's kneeling between my thighs. Gripping the sides of my panties, he pulls them down my legs, dropping them off the side of the bed.

As he runs his hands up the backs of my legs to the swell of my hips, his hungry gaze travels up my body and lands on my eyes. He palms my curves and lifts me slightly, lowering his head. I gasp, realizing what he's going to do and tangle my fingers in his hair, urging him on. Daniel groans before kissing a trail up the inside of my thigh. I tense as he slowly gets closer and closer to my core. I feel mad with lust. I pull at him, clawing him, breathing so fast that I might faint. I plead with him, begging him to do it, over and over again.

He lifts his eyes to mine as he teasingly drags his tongue across my flesh. The feeling is heaven and sin and sex. I'm ready to scream. Clutching the bed sheets, I hold on tight as his lips come into contact with mine. His tongue sweeps between, licking me. He circles the most sensitive part, once, then twice, before taking it between his lips and sucking gently. If he weren't already holding me up, I would fall. The sensations shooting through my body are like an explosion. I can't stand it and Daniel holds me so tightly that I can't move. There's no way to sate my lust, not until he allows me. I can't get away and I can't get any closer. The fact that he's staring into my eyes while he kisses me makes everything that much more intense, and it only takes a few more motions of his tongue before I'm exploding against his mouth, and screaming his name.

Chapter 21

When I come back down, he's released my hips onto the bed and removed his jeans, leaving him in only a pair of snuggly fitting black boxers. I watch him as he lowers those as well, allowing me to see all of him for the first time. I feel amazingly and completely sated, but the sight of his naked body ratchets my need back up to flaming territory. Holy fuck, this man is beautiful! My eyes roam lower and I see gashes running up his legs. My smile fades.

Daniel's face grows hesitant. "Don't feel sorry for me. It was a long time ago."

"Do they still hurt?" The scars wrap around to the front of him in some spots.

He shakes his head. "No, but they're more sensitive than the rest of my legs. I'm not sure why."

Glancing up at him, I ask, "Do you trust me?" He watches me for a moment and I know he's worried. I ask again, "Do you trust me?" I hold out my hand for him, and he takes it. I stand, pulling him toward me and then drop to my knees. One scar is in front of my eyes, along with his gorgeous length. I wait for him to speak.

He finally says, "I trust you." But the words are so soft that I know he's worried.

I press my mouth to the scar and kiss it slowly, sliding my tongue along the marred skin. Daniel sucks in a jagged breath and nearly falls over. He calls out my name and then clutches my head in his hands, leads me back when I pull away. "Please, do it again."

"Did it hurt you?"

"No, it feels—I don't know—it's hard to describe, but I feel your lips on me and it's intense."

"Lay down, then." I smile at him and pull him over to the bed. Daniel looks a little bit shaken. I kiss his temple before

SECOND CHANCES

rolling him onto his stomach. The worst scars are on the back of his legs, down by his knees. It's a tender spot anyway, but add in the scar and it's incredibly sensitive. It's a spot that I love getting kissed. I thought the scars might heighten the sensation for him, and I'm glad that's what happened. I wish I could kiss these away, but since I can't, this is the next best thing.

I crawl on top of his legs as Daniel grabs a pillow in his arms and holds on tight. I lower my head and start to kiss his scars, one by one, tracing them with my tongue and being so gentle that my touch is barely there. Dan's hips slam down into the bed as he writhes. "Holy fuck, Gen!" I do it again, and again. Then I trace the scar that wraps around to his front and roll him over, kissing it and beyond. My mouth makes a beeline for his hard length. Daniel is trembling and his voice comes out shaky, but he stops me. "No, not that way. Not this time."

"I love you, Daniel."

"I know you do. I can tell. Every kiss is…oh, my god, Gen."

Before I can utter a word, he flips me on my back and crawls over me, placing himself between my legs. I spread my knees and rise up, wanting him. Daniel locks his body just above mine, out of reach, and pins me to the bed. Taking my face in his hands, he leans down and brushes his lips across mine once, twice, and on the third pass the kiss deepens and I can taste myself on his tongue. I grip his arms tightly, keeping him close, trying to pull him to me, until I'm forced to let him go.

Daniel turns away and picks up a condom I didn't even see him place on the bed and quickly sheaths himself before placing a hand under each of my thighs and spreading them wider. He keeps his gaze on mine as he slowly slips inside me. By the time his body is flush against mine I'm gasping for air. It's been so long since I've had this with anyone and I've missed being intimate. In this moment, I'm everything to him.

He stays still after he's inside of me, silently asking if I'm okay. Instead of answering him, I move my hips, trying to get him to push back. Daniel slides out

SECOND CHANCES

slowly, almost leaving me completely before he slams back into me. I cry out as he hits every pleasurable spot inside. He begins to move faster and I can tell he's getting close, his thrusts speeding up and becoming more erratic.

Daniel runs his hands across my skin, paying special attention to my nipples, palming my breasts, teasing them with his fingers. He pulls each nipple between his thumb and forefinger rolling them into stiff points as my cries escalate. When I'm gasping for breath and arching my back, desperately pressing my chest closer to him, he leans down to pull each one into his mouth, sucking hard and nipping me gently. His other hand travels down my stomach to the spot between my legs that will push me over the top.

Keeping his hand between my legs, Daniel uses his thumb and presses against my most sensitive part. He begins to alternate his touches, between pressing, pinching, and teasing me by tracing a circle. He watches my face as he tries each thing, taking note of which touch ignites me further. His touch speeds up as he lets my nipple slip from his mouth. He leans back and directs my legs around his waist. I lock my ankles together and give him complete control of our movements.

After just a few more circuits of his thumb, I'm spiraling over the edge, clenching him tightly inside me and bringing him to his own climax. He shouts my name and finds his release, collapsing on top of me. We're both breathing hard, our bodies slick with sweat.

After a few minutes, he raises himself up on his hands and slides out of me. He kisses me softly before getting off the bed and walking to the bathroom, completely naked and comfortable with it. It's the first time I've seen his naked ass, and oh my god, what a nice butt it is. I stare until he shuts the bathroom door, then lay back down to stare at the ceiling.

Chapter 22

Daniel comes back to bed, laying down beside me and tugging me close, cradling me in his arms. He laces our hands together on my stomach and kisses my shoulder softly. I relax into his embrace, and he murmurs, "Are you okay, Baby?"

I smile. "I'm so much better than okay, Daniel." I feel his chuckle against my skin as he huffs out a breath.

"Good." We're both quiet, enjoying just being together, something I didn't think would ever happen again. I realize just how much I missed this, and it was so much more than I remembered. Being in his embrace makes me feel safe, which is something I need after tonight's event. I feel like I'm where I'm supposed to be.

"Daniel?" I ask timidly, afraid to disrupt the happiness I'm feeling, but needing to know. I need to know why he kept us apart when he didn't need to. If he'd only given me a chance, I could have ended all the pain we were both feeling.

"Hmm?" He sounds completely content, and maybe even halfway to sleep, but when I turn in his arms to face him, his eyes fly open and he stares down at me, his eyes full of concern.

Biting my lip, I study his sleepy face. "Why didn't you let me explain? You kept pushing me away, but I don't understand." My voice is small, and trembles slightly. I'm terrified of what his answer might be, and I instantly wish I'd left it alone.

Daniel sighs deeply, his eyes filling with regret. "I was afraid, Genevieve, and hurt." He's not looking at me anymore, instead he's playing with my fingers, and it's so endearing. "You already know that I grew up with my dad, and that my mom left when I was little. My dad wasn't really the touchy-feely kind of dad when he was in a good mood, and I already told you what he did when I caught the tail end of his bad mood. He didn't tell me when I did something good, he only focused on what I did wrong, telling me constantly what I needed to do in order to be better." As I listen to him talk, tears are tracking down my cheeks and into my hair.

"When your husband hired me, I was just a stupid kid. I was taking care of my sister all the time, and resentful of my father. I wanted to get away from him as fast as possible. Cade recognized that in me and spent a lot of time talking to me." He takes a deep breath, closing his eyes as he confesses, "The first time I met you, I couldn't take my eyes off you. You were so beautiful. When Cade introduced us, you smiled at me and shook my hand like I was a man instead of a kid, and after that day, you always brought me a drink or a snack when I was working. I fell in love with you a little more each time you spoke."

"Being around you and Cade was so different from what I was used to. I think in some ways, I loved you just because of how obvious it was that you loved Cade. You never hesitated to tell him. There were times when you would come outside to talk to us and you would just lay a hand on his arm, or wrap your arm around his waist. It was something completely natural for you, and when I saw how he was with you, I wanted to have that too. And, I wanted to have it with you."

He offers a deprecating smile, "Cade knew how I felt about you." This is a side of Cade that I didn't even know about. I can't speak, the knot in my throat is entirely too big.

Daniel keeps talking, telling me things I'd never noticed. "One day, Cade was showing me how to do something, I don't remember what it was, but you came out in another pair of tiny shorts and a tight t-shirt to bring us cold drinks. My tongue practically fell out of my mouth. Cade started laughing, and I was sure he was going to kick my ass. He didn't though, he just said, 'She's beautiful isn't she? I've been in love with that girl my whole life and I'm going to love her forever.' I envied him so much right then, not just for being so sure about his future, but because he was going to get to have you in it."

Raising his eyes to mine, he reaches a hand up to wipe the tears from my cheeks. "Now, I understand completely how it feels to be loved like that. I never thought I would ever have this—I never thought I'd have it with you, Genevieve. I'll never take you for granted. If you'll let me, I'll spend the rest of my life showing you how much I love you and CJ. Not seeing him for the past few weeks has been hell. I adore him every bit as much as I adore you. I can't stand being away from him…or you."

His voice and gaze are full of sincerity, and I throw my arms around his neck, burying my head in his throat. "I love you too Daniel, so, so much!" I can't stop the sobs now. I thought CJ and I would be alone forever. I never thought there would be someone to comfort us and share our lives with. And now that it's happened, it feels unreal.

"I love you, Genevieve," he says tenderly. Then he pulls back, searching my eyes intensely. "But, are you sure about this, about me? You don't feel like I'm trying to take Cade's place, do you? Because I wouldn't want that. I can't imagine how hard this has been for you, I just want to be with you—however you'll have me."

He looks so worried. Placing a hand on his cheek, I stroke his jaw. "I'm absolutely sure, Daniel. And you're right, I did love Cade, and I will always love Cade—he was my first love and the father of my child—but he's not here anymore.

"I don't love you because you knew my husband. I love you because of you, because of who you are. You're a good man and you've been there for me when I felt like I had no one. You never pushed me for anything, you never pressured me. You've always helped, and when I realized I had feelings for you, I was terrified. You're so much younger than I am. I was worried you wouldn't think I was good enough, but you make me feel beautiful everyday, every time I see you. You and Cade are completely different people, and I know that. I love you... for you."

Daniel's eyes mist over before he closes them. He leans in quickly and touches his lips to mine. Just like every other time we've

SECOND CHANCES

kissed, it escalates quickly and soon he's rolled me over again, settling his body on top of mine.

Chapter 23

It's much later when we finally settle down to go to sleep. Using Daniel's phone, I send a quick text to my mother letting her know that I'm not coming home tonight, and that I'm safe. I know when I go home in the morning I'll have a ton of explaining to do, not just about Daniel.

"Would you please turn your brain off and go to sleep?" Daniel's low voice is full of laughter and I can feel the rumble of it as I lie next to him with my head on his chest.

My eyes are already closed, but I pinch him in retaliation, causing him to flinch. "I am." He really does laugh out loud now. But, even as he's laughing, he pulls me

SECOND CHANCES

closer to him, determined to hold me tight. Shutting off my thoughts is much easier said than done though. All I can think about is what's going to happen next. I'm worried about how my mom is going to react at the news that we are really together, and I'm worried about what other people are going to say.

No one seems to have a problem if it's the guy who's ten years older, but when it's a woman? She's called a cougar and made to feel like she's paying a younger guy to be with her. People can be harsh, and very unforgiving.

"Seriously, Genevieve," Daniel groans beside me, "I can practically hear you thinking. What's going on in that head of yours?" He yawns, obviously ready to go to sleep, and I love that even though he's tired he won't go to sleep until he's sure I'm ready to drift off too.

I bite my bottom lip, unsure how to bring it up. He doesn't say anything, choosing to let me work up to it instead, and that gives me the courage to say what I'm thinking. "I'm worried about tomorrow."

"What about it?" I can feel the words rumble through his chest as he speaks. I'm trying to avoid looking at him, so I start making small circles on his left pec, staring at the path my fingers are taking instead of looking directly at him.

I take a deep breath, deciding it's better to just blurt it out and have it be said than trying to soften the blow. "I'm worried about how the conversation with my mom is going to go. She already broke us up once, already. What happens if she tries to do it again? She's the kind of person who will throw out an ultimatum if she feels she has to. I don't want to be in that spot. I can't lose either of you."

"Baby," Daniel says with a sigh, "no matter what she says, I'm not going to leave you. It might make me an asshole, but I really don't care what your mom thinks about our relationship, or me. What's going on between us is just that, between us. Her opinion on it doesn't matter."

That, right there. That's one of the many, many reasons I fell in love with him. Daniel is who he is, regardless of what others think. He's honest and caring, but unlike me, he doesn't let people walk all over him. I wish I could be more like him – maybe I can learn by osmosis? I slide an arm around his waist, hugging him tightly and burying my face in his chest. "Thank you," I tell him, my voice muffled by his skin. "I hate fighting with you."

"I hate fighting with you, too. But, I do have to say that I like making up with you. That was awesome." I don't even have to look up at him to know that he's smirking down at me. I'm sure it's an adorable smirk, too. I laugh lightly before finally settling down to sleep, content with the knowledge that no matter what happens tomorrow, he'll be with me and he won't leave me.

"Goodnight, Daniel," I say, my voice already sounding drowsy.

He kisses the top of my head before saying, "'Night, Baby. Sweet dreams." A small smile curves my lips because I know that being here, in his arms, pretty much guarantees I'm going to have sweet dreams.

Chapter 24

When I wake the following morning, Daniel has one arm beneath me while using his other hand to stroke my arm with the tips of his fingers. Goosebumps raise along the trail and I can feel his erection against my bottom. He presses a kiss to my neck, "Good morning, baby." His voice is still husky from sleep, so he hasn't been awake very long.

"Mmm, morning," I mutter as I stretch, feeling sore thanks to muscles that haven't been used in awhile.

Daniel moves my hair away from my face so that he can place a soft kiss in the spot where my neck meets my shoulder and

SECOND CHANCES

I tremble slightly. Chuckling against me, he says, "I should probably get you home, huh?"

Oh man. I don't even want to think about how that's going to go. "Yeah, I should probably get home. I'm sure Mom is ready to hand CJ off."

When we leave Daniel's apartment, he links our fingers together, tugging me close to him as we walk down to his truck. The only time he lets go of my hand is after he helps me into the seat. He closes my door and heads over to the driver's side. As soon as he climbs in, he takes my hand again and I scoot over to cuddle up to his side. Having a relationship with someone is strange after more than two years of being alone. I don't want to be far from him.

He doesn't say much on the drive, but the closer we get, the tenser he becomes. I know he's worrying about how I'm going to react to what Mom will say, but I don't know how to reassure him. I just know that I have to at least try.

"Hey," I say, tipping my head up to look at him. "She can't say anything that will change how I feel about you, okay? I know you, and I know the truth. Whatever she thinks doesn't matter."

Daniel sighs, shaking his head. "Genevieve, you know that's not true. She's your mom, and no matter what, her opinion does matter to you. She's the only family you have left and I won't be responsible for taking that away from you."

My heart swells in my chest at his words. He really does understand me. Leaning my head against his shoulder, I enjoy the closeness we have and pray that my mother doesn't try to take this away from us.

When we pull up outside of my house, I watch my mother pull the curtains to the side, and her reaction at seeing Daniel help me out of his truck is everything I thought it would be. Her eyes narrow and she drops the curtain. Ten seconds later, she comes storming out the front door, a pissed-off expression on her face.

Rushing forward, I meet her on the walkway before she can get to Daniel. "Mom," I implore, "please, can we go inside and talk about this? I don't want the neighbors to hear all of this."

SECOND CHANCES

"Hmpf. Yes, let's go inside. When you left last night, I had no idea you were going to see him." She says with such disdain, and I can't figure out what he ever did to her. "If I'd known you were going to meet up with him, I would never have agreed to watch CJ. I'm so disappointed in you, Genny Prior."

I tip my head to the side and feel the person I've become finally emerge. I'm not taking this anymore. Hands on my hips, I spurt out, "Yeah, well, I'm disappointed in you too, Mom."

Her eyes flash up to mine, surprise and disbelief prominently displayed on her face. I'm expecting her to completely fly off the handle, but instead she just turns on her heel and walks back into the house, saying nothing to Daniel or me.

Turning, I motion to Daniel to come on and he walks up to meet me. Taking his hand, I lead him into the house, intent on having this out with my mother. She needs to understand that Daniel isn't going anywhere and that I won't let her influence my relationship, no matter how much I love her.

Once we are all inside, she turns to face us, crossing her arms over her chest and staring us both down. "Well, Genevieve, do you have anything to say for yourself?" Her tone is caustic, but I can hear an undertone of hurt there as well.

Pinching the bridge of my nose, I try to figure out a way to have this conversation with her without it starting a huge fight. I can feel Daniel at my back, he's trying to support me, to show my mom that we are a united front, although I'm not sure it's going to do any good. "What would you like me to say Mother? I asked you over here last night because I needed to go talk to Daniel. If I told you my plans, you wouldn't have come."

"You're right," she agrees with a nod, "I wouldn't have. I also wouldn't have volunteered to be your babysitter so you could go act like a teenage girl instead of the thirty-three-year-old woman you really are—you're too old for him." She has her hands on her hips as she reads me the riot act and I'm trying hard not to let her words bother me. I can feel Daniel's body tighten with anger as his hand grips mine.

SECOND CHANCES

Looking back at him, I give him what I hope is a reassuring smile before turning back to my mom. "Mom, I love you, you know that I do, but you're wrong about him! I don't understand why you're so against this. He's been making sure things around this house have been taken care of since before Cade left on his deployment. He's been nothing but respectful to you and to me. I just don't get it!"

"When are you going to realize that he's only here because he thinks you will be his sugar mama?" She says the last two words like she walks around talking street, day and night. Then she deflates right in front of me, her eyes sad instead of angry. "I just don't want to see you get hurt. I didn't think you would ever get over Cade, and now, you've moved on to this young man who doesn't know the first thing about living in the real world—"

Daniel's control has come to an end. He steps in front of me protectively, ending her tirade. "First of all, how dare you think that the only reason I would be with your daughter is because she has money. How dare you!" My mom's eyes widen at his words, and truthfully, so do mine. "I don't need Gen's money. I have a trust fund of my own. And yeah, I could have had it very easy by going to work for my father, but I'm not interested in his business, and, frankly, I don't want anything to do with him. As soon as I can pull my sister out of his house, I will.

"Do you see this?" He jerks up the leg of his pants, tugging his jeans high enough to reveal the scars. "The man you admire so much whipped his own seven-year-old. I don't want to be like him. I don't want anything to do with him. There's a reason my mother left, and I don't blame her."

Daniel watches my mother's face as it shifts from anger to horror. He pauses for a second, shaking his jeans back down to his ankle. "Listen, I want to make my own way, my own fortune. I want to sink or swim on my own, not succeed just because of who my father is, and if my business went under tomorrow, I'd still be able to take care of Genevieve and your grandson without touching her money at all. I have more money than I could ever spend, invested in more stocks and bonds than you could count. This isn't about money, so stop acting like it is." He stops to take a breath, and my mother looks on in shock, still speechless at everything he's saying.

"With all due respect, Mrs. Howlett, I love your daughter and your grandson. I respected Cade when he was alive, and I'm damn sure not going to disrespect him now by taking advantage of his widow." He's standing tall in front of me when he finishes, and when I look around him at my mother; she has tears in her eyes and is looking at him with grudging respect.

Daniel pulls me to him, wrapping an arm around my waist and pulling me into his side. He's staring my mother down, but her face says she finally understands what I see in him. She is realizing she doesn't know everything about him—that Daniel isn't who she thought he was.

She walks over to us, taking my face in her hands and kissing my cheek before hugging me tightly. "I'm wrong and I'm sorry," she says softly into my hair. I nod, and she pulls away to do the same to him. I can feel him stiffen when she motions for him to bend over because he's too tall for her to grab his cheeks. I don't know what she says into his ear, but whatever it is must've been good since he relaxes against me.

My mom looks like a huge weight has been taken off her shoulders and I suddenly realize how hard watching me grieve for Cade has been on her. It explains why she was always pushing me towards guys that she thought could take care of me, and why she was so against Daniel in the beginning. To someone who doesn't know him, he must look like a young kid who's just experimenting. I know now that she was just trying to protect me, even if she went about it wrong.

A single tear rolls down her cheek and she brushes it away. "I'm going to go. I've got so much to do at home, and I'm sure the three of you want to spend time together." She kisses my cheek once more before walking out the front door, leaving me to watch her with my mouth gaping open.

The door shuts and Daniel turns to me with a grin. "Well, that went way better than I was expecting."

SECOND CHANCES

"I was a little worried."

Daniel snorts, "A little? I was a lot worried. Gen, your mom is scary."

"You handled her pretty well though." I feel almost giddy at the thought that my mom seems to be on board with our relationship. I don't want to fight with her, but there's no way I'm giving Daniel up, either.

Pulling me over to the couch, Daniel sits down beside me, tucking me into his side. "Now that I've faced the firing squad and won, can we relax for a few before CJ gets up from his nap? I just want to enjoy the fact that we can be together."

Giggling at his analogy, I nod. He's absolutely right. Not having to hide the fact that we're in love is freeing. I snuggle closer as he turns on the television, searching for something to watch and enjoying his company.

Chapter 25

Daniel and I quickly settle into a routine, one that involves him spending the majority of his time at my house instead of his apartment. That doesn't mean that life after the confrontation with my mom is all sunshine and roses, though. Today is the first time I'll see Lanie and Maggie with Daniel as my boyfriend instead of just *the guy who mows my lawn*, and I have a feeling things won't go very smoothly. It's confirmed when Lanie starts in on me as soon as she walks in.

"Are you nuts?" asks Lanie, her voice almost squeaking it goes so high.

SECOND CHANCES

Shaking my head, I give her a dirty look. "No, I'm not nuts, but thanks for that."

"I'm serious, Genny! It's one thing to have sex with the younger guy, but to publicly date him? What are you thinking?" She's looking at me like she's not sure she ever really knew me, which kinda hurts. I expect this kind of thing from my mom, but not my best friend. "Do you really want everyone to think you're a cougar, or his sugar mama?"

I open my mouth to let her have it, but Daniel's voice cuts me off as his arm wraps protectively around my waist and I relax into his body. Even with my friend acting like someone I don't know, he makes me feel safe and protected. "You know, I'm getting really tired of people who supposedly want the best for Genevieve, the people who are supposed to know her better than anyone else, thinking that there has to be an ulterior reason I'm with her. Why can't any of you see the woman that I see?"

He tugs me further into his embrace as he continues to blast my friend. "Gen is an amazing person and any man, young or old would be lucky to have her. I can promise you now that I will never take her for granted and I will always do everything I can to be what she needs." Lanie's eyes widen at his words, and her eyes fill with tears when he tells her, "If you can't respect her or our relationship, please leave."

I'm speechless. No one has ever seen me the way he does, and it's a heady feeling. My friends are staring at him like he's sprouted an extra head, and they aren't sure how to respond to his words. Neither one of them can really argue with him. I melt at the way he protects me, and so do my friends.

Then, Lanie's eyes meet mine, and I can see the sadness in them. She rushes over to throw her arms around me, burying her head in my shoulder and whispering, "Oh God, I'm so sorry. I wasn't thinking! You know I love you more than anything, right?" Daniel doesn't release me at first, and I appreciate that he's trying to protect me, but this is a girl I've been friends with since we were kids.

SECOND CHANCES

"It's okay," I comfort Lanie, hugging her back tightly as Maggie comes over to hug us both. Daniel finally lets me go so that I can hug it out with the two people I'm closest to, after him.

He leaves the living room, giving us our privacy. Once the three of us have cried, apologized, and reiterated that we love each other dearly, he walks back in holding a bottle of wine and three glasses. He pours us each a glass before kissing me sweetly.

"I'm going to give you some time with your friends, baby. Call when you're ready for me to come back, okay?"

God, I love this man! I kiss him, assuring him we'll be ready soon. After all, I'm not going to spend the whole night with my friends. I want to see him, too. He's been busy with school this week, so we haven't spent as much time together.

The three of us watch him leave before Lanie turns to me and squeals, "Okay, now that he's gone, I seriously need details!" Grabbing me by the arm, careful not to spill the freshly poured glass of wine she handed me, she drags me over to the couch and pushes me down, sitting beside me. "How long has this been going on, Genny?"

"About two weeks." I cringe, knowing she's going to shriek any minute. Lanie doesn't disappoint, her squeals are almost deafening in their intensity.

"What do you mean, two weeks?! Why didn't you say anything?" Maggie sounds hurt.

When I look over at her, I raise a single eyebrow. A blush blooms across her cheeks. "Oh, yeah, I guess tonight is why."

"Partly," I nod. "I was afraid you wouldn't understand, but I also wanted to just keep it to myself for a little while." I tell them about my mom's reaction, and how I was at the bar Daniel had been working at the night my car was almost stolen. I hadn't told them that I'd gone to see him, or that he'd been the one to give me a ride home.

Lanie snickers, "I guess he really did give you a ride, huh?" My face flames at her words and I swear I can feel the blush all the way down to my toes as I smack her in the arm.

SECOND CHANCES

"Shut up, Lanie! Jeez." I can't stay mad at these girls, it's downright impossible—and has been that way since we were little.

We spend the rest of the night talking about Daniel, our getting together, and my mother's reaction, which makes Maggie laugh. "I knew she would freak if y'all worked things out! Your mom is so crazy!"

At one point, Lanie leans forward to ask me, "So, now you have to tell me—did Mr. Handyman teach you how to screw?" Maggie and I both spit out our wine at her ridiculous question. When we both look at her in shock, she shrugs. "Hey, I was there that day when we ogled him putting up the new chandelier. The guy knows how to screw, I just want to know if he taught you anything new!"

Maggie and I both collapse into the couch, laughing at her serious expression. The girl is absolutely crazy. When I don't answer, she glares at me. "What?" I ask, even though I know exactly what she wants to know.

"Are you going to answer me or not? Inquiring minds want to know!" She's getting ticked now at my lack of answers, so I decide to take pity on her.

"He's definitely taught me some things. Did you know that young guys have some serious stamina? It's amazing." Honestly, it's been so long since I had sex that I probably wouldn't know if he did have more stamina than a guy my age. I just want to see her face at the revelation. Lanie does not disappoint.

Her mouth drops open and her eyes glaze over. "Really? Does Daniel have any friends he can hook me up with?"

Maggie's husband comes to pick them up around ten, and just as they are getting ready to leave, Daniel gets back. Walking past him, Lanie cups his cheek in her hand, leaning up to say something in his ear. He smiles at her and nods before she kisses his cheek and follows Maggie out the door.

As soon as the door shuts, he walks over to kiss me. I pull back to study him, and his brows furrow. "What is it?" he asks.

"What did Lanie just say to you?" It must not have been bad because he just grinned down at her, but I'm so curious, I almost can't stand it.

SECOND CHANCES

He shakes his head, a small smile still present on his lips. "Oh, that?" I narrow my eyes at him and he pulls me into his embrace. "She was just warning me that if I hurt you, I'll have to deal with her. Your friend is very inventive with her revenge techniques." He's laughing now, but refuses to tell me what she said she'd do to him, telling me I'll have to ask her.

Daniel helps me clean up before taking my hand and leading me up to my room. It's crazy to think that we are just starting to be open with other people about our relationship, because being with him is as natural as breathing. We both undress, getting ready for bed and slipping underneath the covers.

I turn to face away from him, and he yanks me over so that I'm cuddled up against him, keeping his arm possessively around my waist. I feel his lips touch the top of my head, in what's quickly become our nightly ritual.

"Sweet dreams, baby," he says.

My eyes are heavy, and I'm almost asleep, so I don't even know if he hears my whispered, "Good night, Daniel." I feel safe with him lying here beside me, and I'm comfortable enough to fall asleep quickly, secure in the knowledge that he'll still be here when I wake up tomorrow.

A few months ago, I never would have thought this could happen. I'm starting a new life with someone. I'm actually moving forward. I will always love Cade, but I love Daniel too. I didn't think I'd be able to love anyone ever again, but that isn't true. It's liberating to be free from my tear-filled nights and thoughts of enduring parenthood. Being a single parent was one of the hardest things I've had to do, but I managed. Now, I've been given a second chance at love—and I'm taking it.

THE END

Free Sample:

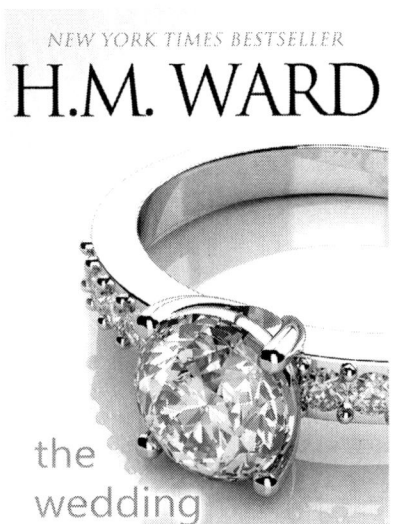

THE WEDDING CONTRACT

Chapter 1

I can hear Amy's voice through the front wall of the little shop, talking to a potential client about photography for their wedding. I'm in the back, putting away props from this morning's shoot. After stowing the box on a shelf in the back, I walk across the open space, and duck out through the curtain that covers the doorway to the front.

"Well, congratulations, and thank you for considering Bella Chicks Studio. Best of luck to you both." Amy smiles as she sets the phone back into the cradle. Her light brown hair is pin straight and tied back into a style that looks perfect on her. When I try it, my curls just look tangled.

Folding my arms over my chest, I breathe in slowly. It's stupid to think that this was his doing. Amy hasn't even told me yet, but the skin on my arms prickles like a big fat omen. I know it was him. It's always him. "So, I take it the Gettys hired someone else?"

Amy smiles at me. It's the facial expression that begs, 'Don't kill the messenger!' I'm not mad at Amy; I'm upset about the situation. We can't keep losing clients like this. She nods slowly. "Yeah, they went with Bella Clicks."

My lips smash together and I try not to yell. I try so hard not to overreact, but this is the third client that Nick Ferro has stolen from me this month. The bastard has been making my eye twitch for weeks. It seems like every time I figure out how to get a step ahead of him, he one-ups me, and then does it better and cheaper. God, I hate him.

The worst part is, if things continue like this, I can't afford to stay in my little shop. Babylon Village is cute, but the rent is a bitch. And I know Mr. Copycat doesn't have that issue because his daddy owns the damn shopping center. Why didn't I get a non-compete clause in my lease contract?

Amy can tell that my blood is boiling. "Uh, Sky. You haven't blinked in like, five minutes. Don't go all Medusa on me." Amy is a mythology buff and works

Greek gods into anything and everything. Half the time I don't even know what she's talking about.

The ringing in my ears should be my cue to go scream in the back room like a normal small business owner. Instead, I knot my tightly folded arms and shove through the glass front door. My feet pound the parking lot, hard and fast, leaving Amy and her don't-do-its behind.

This has to stop. I was doing fine until Nick showed up. God knows there are enough people trying to make a living in New York, but none of them, aside from this ass-hat, camped out on my doorstep stealing my clients.

I never do stuff like this. I never chew anyone out. I always smile and look for the bright side of things. Screw that. I'll be out of business if I don't fight back, so I shove into his store, my fists up and fangs bared.

"Get out of here, you sorry excuse for a man!" I'm standing in his perfect lobby, which is just as posh as mine, but instead of rich red accents, his are blue. He has his consultation table in the same spot as mine, with huge pictures of brides in Time Square and by Saint Pat's Cathedral, just like I do. I notice the new floral arrangements with peacock feathers, and I'm ready to explode. When did he copy those?

My eyes drift over to the little table he has set up with albums on it. Last month, I met a new vendor that provides these beautiful albums for my boudoir clients. The albums have sequins, supple leather, and feel perfect under your fingertips. I see one glinting from behind a wedding album on his table. Wide-eyed, I step toward it and lift the little book with shaking hands.

Nick appears from the back and shakes his head slowly. "Sky Thompson, what can I do for you?" Nick has dark, perfectly tousled hair that falls over his forehead, right above gem-colored blue eyes. Today, he's wearing a designer white button-down shirt with jeans. There's a chunky watch on his wrist that cost more than my net worth. He's beautiful, cocky, and rich. His voice is like a siren's song, and he completely and totally sucks rabid monkeys—a spoiled brat to the core.

Anger surges through me, as I look up at him. "What'd you do to land the Getty wedding? Offer to pose with her in the boudoir pictures?" Oh my god. Nick has the audacity to smile while I'm ranting. He tries to hide it, but I can see the amusement in his eyes. I shove a finger into his chest and continue raving. "Because there's no way you could get that client on your own, you pampered ass!"

Nick looks like he's biting the inside of his mouth to keep from laughing. I'm right in front of him and seriously consider kicking his shins. Every muscle in my body is strung so tight that I'm ready to explode. I'm practically vibrating—until I see Beverly Getty emerge from the back room, followed by her daughter and husband. Awh, suck.

I deflate as I see the livid look on Beverly's face. She told me that she'd be sending a check today, but she's in Nick's studio instead. I don't get it, and from the look on her face, she doesn't plan to elaborate. "What did you say about my daughter? Or was your crass comment directed at me, Miss Thompson?"

What the fuckery? Seriously, I never blow off steam! I never tell anyone that they suck and the one time I do, it bites me on the ass. My lips tug into a nervous smile and I have that weird feeling where I don't know what to do with my hands. I grab my pointer finger and try to patch things up, like I didn't just eat my foot. No, I swallowed my whole damn leg and half my ass. There's no way to make this right. "Mrs. Getty, I didn't mean to imply—"

"You didn't imply anything, dear. And if you must know, we found Nick to be much more easygoing. A wedding is stressful enough and I didn't want anything else to make my Tiffany anxious. I see I chose well and I'll make sure that everyone knows how you really behave."

Nick glances between us before putting a hand on Beverly's shoulder. "Sky wouldn't have ruined your daughter's wedding. She's a very capable photographer. The truth is, she only gets twitchy like this when she forgets her meds. It could happen to anyone." Beverly Getty gives me a second look, like she can now see my obvious mental defect.

"Go back and grab a chai tea from the Keurig. I'll get those new albums I mentioned." He looks up at me and grins. "On your way, Sky. Or would you prefer I call Amy to fetch you?" He says it so sweetly, as if he's helping me.

Not meaning to, I clutch my hands tightly and growl before I turn on my heel and storm out. As the door closes behind me, I hear Nick saying to the Gettys, "Don't worry, she's not dangerous."

Chapter 2

Amy is standing in the doorway when I get back. My eyes are stinging and I want to cry. I go straight into the back and she trails behind me like a faithful puppy. "Sky, what happened? It can't be that bad!"

"I called Tiffany Getty a slut and suggested that the only reason they signed with Nick was to touch his naked chest!" I'm sniffling hard, trying not to cry—not before I find the tissue box. I head over to the prop shelves and start digging around. A crate of plastic apples topples off the shelf, onto the floor, spilling apples in every direction.

"Well, that's not that bad." She has a quizzical tone to her voice that tells me she doesn't understand.

"The Gettys were there! All three of them walked out from the back of his shop. Her dad looked like he wanted to slit my throat and toss me into the canal."

Amy averts her eyes. "Oh, well, yeah. That's kinda bad."

I find the little tissue box and sink to the floor. "That's not the worst part. Nick told them that I'm usually fine—that I only get like this when I forget my meds. So I went from being a bitch to being crazy!" Holding the tissue over my face, I take a deep breath. I need to calm down, but I can't.

"Oh, honey. It's okay. It's all going to be okay." She kneels next to me and rubs my shoulder.

"How can you say that? He's ruined me. My business is falling apart because of him. The guy is a parasite and you're telling me that it's all okay?" I'm not usually like this. I don't fall to pieces over little things, but it's so far past little that I can't take it anymore. I went from having a thriving shop to sneak-sleeping in the store. I have no apartment, no money, and thanks to Nick, I lost the Getty wedding.

"Of course it's okay. Everyone knew you were crazy already." She smiles and leans in, giving me a hug.

"Gee, thanks."

"Seriously, Sky. Cut yourself some slack. You won't close with every client. Some of them will choose someone else. You can't beat yourself up when one gets away." She only says that because she doesn't know how bad it is. I've been hiding it from her. Amy has enough stuff to worry about, I haven't wanted to add more to her pile.

But it's going to become very obvious, very soon. I clutch my face and don't look up. My gaze is fixated on the floor. "Go look at the calendar. My close-rate got cut in half after the ass-hat moved in. Clients walk out of here with my packet in hand, and I swear to God that he looks it over, offers them the same coverage for less money, and then gives them an extra album. I don't even have a chance."

Amy continues to encourage me. "Sky, you're better than him. You're the one who comes up with the newest ideas."

"But, Amy, a week later, he has them, too!"

"Do you remember that Trash-the-Dress session in the city? It was so much fun. And you have another client thinking about booking a similar session. Don't let him get you down. There will always be people trying to get a piece of what you have, Sky, because you're the best. They want to be you."

Her words calm me down enough to look up. She smiles and hands me one of the fancy mirrors we use in pin-up shoots. "It looks like a dog licked your face."

My mascara is running down my cheeks and a big smear of eye shadow looks like dirt on my temple. The corner of my mouth twitches.

"Sky," Amy begins, "you have a new idea, don't you?"

"Yeah." I stare into the glass, my imagination running wild. The picture hasn't fully formed in my mind yet, but I can see the client in the water, make-up darkened and smeared. Something unusual and tragic. It's like nothing I've ever shot before and very un-bride-like, but amazing all the same.

Amy waves a hand in front of my face to catch my attention. "Hello? Are you going to try it this weekend with Sophie?"

"If she lets me." My eyes flick up over the top of the mirror. "It would be so cool, and Shelter Island is the perfect place to do it." I bite my bottom lip, thinking about the logistics, and hand the mirror back to Amy to be put away.

"I wish I was coming with you. Five days out there sounds awesome—especially at this time of year. I bet it's beautiful." Amy stands and brushes herself off. She usually comes with me to carry gear and help out, but this wedding is small and I'm doing it at cost as a favor to a childhood friend. The only money I'll make is from print sales after the wedding.

I say her new name out loud. "Sophie Stevens. I can't believe she's getting married."

"Yeah, but Stevens is a lot easier to say, am I right?"

"Yeah, Poloiscitiano doesn't exactly roll off the tongue."

Amy resumes her duties at the front desk, preparing paperwork. "Go home, Sky. Pack and take an earlier ferry out. Sit on the beach until Sophie gets there. God knows you could use a break. Just be sure to make fun of her new husband for me. 'Steven Stevens' is too funny." It's a name that sounds like it belongs to a cartoon dog carrying a briefcase.

"Are you sure? There's so much work to do and I feel bad—"

"You always feel bad and you never stop working. You're always here. Go, I'm fine. I can blast sixties music and walk around barefoot." She winks at me, teasing. Amy would dress like a flower child every day of the year. She taps a stack of papers on her desk and staples the corner. "Seriously, go. Have fun. Relax for a few days. Drink champagne and sleep with a stranger. You know, typical wedding stuff."

I laugh. "Typical for you, maybe."

Amy tips her head to the side, like she feels sorry for me. "You're twenty-two, Sky. You bust your ass every day and never stop to see what you're missing."

"Because I'm not missing a thing." I grab my purse from the desk drawer and push it shut. "Are you sure you're good here if I take off?" I never leave work early. If I haul ass, I can make the two o'clock ferry and get there with enough time to spend a few hours walking the beach or looking in the little shops.

Amy smirks, "Only if you promise to nail the best man for me." She waggles her eyebrows and clicks her tongue at me.

"Yeah. I'll do that," I say sarcastically, grabbing a shipping label and a marker from the desk drawer. Quickly, I scrawl, AMY WAS HERE across the envelope. "There ya go. I'll leave it on his forehead."

She laughs. "Bitch."

"No, crazy. I thought we established that."

As I push out the door, Amy yells, "Bring me some cake!"

"Will do!"

Chapter 3

By the time I get to the North Ferry at Orient Point, it's the middle of the afternoon. I change out of the suit I wear at the studio and trade it for a pair of faded jeans with a hole in the knee and a stretchy black tee shirt. I sit on the hood of my crappy old car, Big Red, and pull my dark hair into a ponytail. The wind is whipping it around, making it difficult to see. The truth is, I love the smell of the salt water and I love Shelter Island even more. Sophie's family maintains a summer home there, and since her parents were friends with my parents, we came out here with Sophie a lot. Sophie and I have been best friends since we were little. I don't really want to work her wedding, but she insisted that I do it.

Taking a deep breath, I look around. There are a few cars parked next to me, but since it's not summer anymore, the boat isn't full. Big Red is a rust-colored Bonneville that's older than I am. It sat in my grandpa's garage until he died last year. It's too big for the compact, modern parking spaces and was constructed back when gas was cheap and cars were huge. Grandpa used to complain about it being too small, which seems funny now. Both tires straddle the parking space. I used to have a motorcycle, but I had to sell it to make ends meet last month. Now it's just me and Big Red.

When we make it to the island, I follow the trail of cars off the boat and hit the road. I want to get checked in and make it to the other side of the island before Sophie arrives. I find the little inn that everyone is staying at and manage to parallel park. Who's awesome? Me! Maybe today won't suck after all. Horrible morning means a pleasant evening. I think I read that on a fortune cookie once.

Grabbing my purse, I head inside and go to the check-in counter. A woman with bright red hair and a black blazer is standing there with a phony smile on her clashing red lips.

"Welcome to the Chaucer Inn," she says. "How may I help you?"

God, she looks crazy. Her big green eyes don't blink and that creepy smile remains tightly in place. After glancing quickly around, I decide her boss must be nearby because something is making her uncomfortable and unnaturally still.

Placing my hands on the counter, I say, "Yes, I'm the photographer for the Stevens Wedding. I was told a room was reserved for me."

"Check in time isn't until 4pm."

"I know, but I hoped the room would be ready early. It was a long drive. Do you think you could help me out?"

She rolls her eyes and the smile fades. She breathes deeply, flaring her nostrils like a bull. "I am happy to help you find a seat at our restaurant until 4pm."

Did she not hear me? I tap my finger on the counter and lean in a little bit. "Is there any chance that I can have my room now? I'm really tired and—?"

"No! You can't have it now! It's not ready now! It'll be ready at 4pm! Are you hard of hearing or something?" The woman grips her side of the counter for a second and practically snarls.

Holy snails. That is the face of crazy. I smile with too many teeth and back away slowly. "I'll come back at 4pm."

The woman goes back to her unblinking, pleasantly possessed status. "That's a wonderful idea. Thank you so much. Enjoy your afternoon on Shelter Island."

OMG. What a nutter. I get out of the lobby before she sprouts claws and rips me to shreds. When I'm back out on the street, I decide to walk and grab a late lunch to kill the time. I'm sitting at a little bistro before I finally relax a little. My eye stops twitching, all thoughts of Nick and his assy ways long gone, and I'm content for once, sipping iced tea and nibbling on my sandwich. The little restaurant has all its seating outdoors on the sidewalk. The sky is blue and a slight breeze rustles through the branches. It's perfect.

Until my phone rings. It plays the Imperial March, aka Darth Vader's theme song, signaling that it's my mother calling. The guy next to me snorts his soda and looks over. I give a weak smile and slump back in my chair, letting it play the song again. Glancing at him, I explain, "It's my Mom."

He gives me a crooked grin. "She sounds amazing." The beautiful man returns to his meal with a smile on his face.

I swipe my finger across the screen and hold the evil little device to my ear. "Hey, Mom."

"Are you already out there? What happened at work today? You can't skip out just because you have somewhere fun to be." My mother thinks my job is a joke even though it more than paid the bills until Nick showed up. No one knows just how bad it's gotten and I sure as hell don't want to hear her lectures now.

"Mom, I didn't skip out. Amy is there."

"Amy won't do the same job you would do."

"Amy is stapling papers. I don't think she'll staple her hand too often, so we're okay. Have you and Daddy left yet?"

"Don't change the subject, Missy! I told you that you should have gone to college like Sophie did, but did you listen?

No. Now, you run off in the middle of the day and leave Amy there alone. What if someone wants something?"

"Then they call me on my cell phone." Oh, God. Someone shoot me. I lean my cheek into my hand and lean sideways as Mom chews me out.

"That's no way to run a business, Sweetheart. Have you thought about what Daddy and I offered?"

"I'm not going to close my studio, Ma." My tilted body is off balance, as I perch on the side of my chair, ready to topple over. We've had this conversation too many times to count. They think I threw my life away because I didn't get a college degree. The thing is, all my friends who did are now jobless and flipping burgers. I don't have their debt and things were pretty good until Nick started screwing with me.

"Sophie is going to talk to you and I think you should listen to her."

My feet are crossed at the ankle. When she says that, I push too hard on my right foot and try to sit up quickly, but I must be standing on my shoelaces because my foot doesn't move. So, instead of going up, I fall down.

Picture a penguin at the zoo that suddenly falls sideways. Boop. It's really funny, except when I fall, my hands dart out and grab the closest thing to me—the guy at the next table. I manage to clutch a fist full of crotch and grope him thoroughly before hitting the cement. If he hadn't been facing me with his legs splayed like that, it wouldn't have happened. I was trying to grab the chair and totally missed.

The guy's eyes go wide and he jumps up, bumping the table with his hip. His pasta dish and tea start to slide as gravity pulls everything downward. By this time, I'm on the ground and I turn just in time to get a plate of spaghetti in the face, followed by a full glass of tea to wash it off.

I can hear my mother shrieking from somewhere on the sidewalk, still scolding me. For a moment, no one says anything. They just watch in horrified silence. I wipe the sauce and tea from my face and glance down. It looks like I was the victim of an assassination attempt by a clown. There's a huge red stain over my boobs with limp noodles in my hair, and a few hanging from the neckline of my shirt. One noodle is actually caught in my necklace. The tea diluted the sauce, which then ran into every crevice of my body, so I'm saucy and sticky. Not to mention, I groped a random stranger and knocked his table over.

I sit there way too long, trying to blink the stinging sensation out of my eyes. When I look up, the guy has his hand out. I take it and he helps me up.

"I am so sorry," he says. He isn't laughing at me, which comes as a shock.

"No, it was my fault," I say. Someone hands me my phone and I hit END CALL without telling my mom goodbye. She calls back two seconds later.

Handsome guy chuckles at the Imperial March as it plays again. "I suggest not answering that."

I laugh, otherwise I'd cry. "Not planning on it."

The wait staff bustles around us, righting his table and cleaning up my mess, leaving the two of us standing awkwardly in the middle of the restaurant. "My name's Deegan, by the way. Deegan Greene. I'm a Sci-Fi nerd and I'm pretty sure you're a goddess."

A shy smile passes over my face, as I look at the ground and then back up at him. I hold out my sticky hand. "Sky Thompson."

"Can I walk you back to your hotel, Sky?"

"That depends. Is it four o'clock, yet?"

His jaw drops slightly. "Are you here for the Steve Stevens wedding, too?" The way he says it makes me laugh even though his lunch is stuck to my body.

"Yeah. How'd you know?"

"I'm guessing we had the same receptionist. I'm Steve's best friend."

I nod and pull a piece of spaghetti from my shirt. "I'm the photographer."

"Really?" I don't know why he says it like that. Apparently, I made a really bad impression, as if I'm too clumsy to photograph people.

"Yeah. I've known Sophie since we were kids."

"Ah, well then. We have a lot of catching up to do. I'm pretty sure if we put our heads together, we can thoroughly embarrass them." He winks at me and takes my elbow, before dropping enough cash for both of us on the table. "Steven had an unnatural love of glue. I'd hoped he'd have aspirations to take over the company that makes sticky-notes when he grew up."

I laugh a little. "It must have been a disappointment to see him become a pediatrician."

"Indeed. Come on. Let's see if we can get Satan's Spawn to let us check in. If she refuses, you should go sit on that big white chaise in the center of the lobby. I bet they'll change their mind about that four o'clock policy."

THE WEDDING CONTRACT IS AVAILABLE NOW

New Releases

To ensure you don't miss H.M. Ward's next book, text AWESOMEBOOKS (one word) to 22828 and you will get an email reminder on release day.

*****

Want to talk to other fans?
Go to Facebook and join the discussion!

Coming Soon

BROKEN PROMISES
A Trystan Scott Novel

More Ferro Family Books

NICK FERRO

~THE WEDDING CONTRACT~

*****

BRYAN FERRO

~THE PROPOSITION~

*****

SEAN FERRO

~THE ARRANGEMENT~

******

PETER FERRO GRANZ

~DAMAGED~

******

JONATHAN FERRO

~STRIPPED~

******

TRYSTAN SCOTT

~COLLIDE~

******

More Romance Books by

H.M. Ward

DAMAGED

DAMAGED 2

STRIPPED

SCANDALOUS

SCANDALOUS 2

SECRETS

THE SECRET LIFE OF TRYSTAN SCOTT

And more.

To see a full book list, please visit:
www.SexyAwesomeBooks.com/books.htm

Can't Wait for H.M. Ward's

Next Steamy Book?

Let her know by leaving stars and telling
her what you liked about
Second Chances
in a review!